FLESH

Flesh

BRIGID BROPHY

faber and faber

I. M.

This edition first published in 2013
by Faber and Faber Ltd
Bloomsbury House, 74–77 Great Russell Street
London WC1B 3DA

A CIP record for this book is available from the British Library

ISBN 978-0-571-30468-4

Introduction to the 2013 Edition

In sexual fables of instructor and protégé it is, traditionally, a man who takes the lead and a woman who follows, whether or not wholly willing. Thus Pygmalion and Galatea, George Bernard Shaw's famous variation on same, and so forth. In her third novel *Flesh* (1962), Brigid Brophy turns the tables, without fuss or contrivance, but with great style and acute perception. If women are usually seen, for cosmetic reasons, as the more mutable sex, in *Flesh* it is a man who is transformed, both in body and mind, under a woman's skilful hands. The process of change, though, runs on a little further than either party had quite bargained for.

Marcus, Brophy's male lead, doesn't seem like promising raw material when first we meet him. Awkward and ungainly, carrying the mantle of 'the son in a Jewish family', he cuts a tortured figure at parties – so inwardly hyperaesthetic as to make small talk impossible, his face 'a great ruby and white badge of over-sensitivity, wearing a look of Noli Me Tangere.' Everything about Marcus is wrong in this way – down to the pained, over-thought inadequacy of the flat he can't afford to decorate as he'd like – and all of it Brophy paints in close detail, deftly, just as she does every inch of the novel.

Incredibly, at one more unpromising party Marcus is 'rescued' by a young woman named Nancy, with whom he manages to struggle through a conversation, to express some of his pent-up inner passions, to offer, even, that his favourite painter is Rubens. The effort is epochal for him:

afterward something, clearly, has changed. In short order Marcus will feel 'like a derelict property suddenly bought up by a speculator'. And his mother will be near to tears in 'her joy that Marcus had a girlfriend at last'.

Who is this Nancy, and what is her game? Like Marcus she comes from a solid North West London Jewish family (though hers is a bit more solidly bourgeois). She's keenly intelligent, notably competent, orderly, clear-eyed and candid. With her short, thick black hair and trim figure she is, in Brophy's lovely phrase, like 'the neat black head of a match'. In time she will tell Marcus that she doesn't care to be taken for 'a bullying female'. Nonetheless, without malice, she seems to have looked for a mate whom she can mould.

The first challenges for the would-be couple are how to get clear of the shadows cast by their respective families, and past Marcus's obvious physical repression, too. At a dance thrown for Nancy by her parents she teaches Marcus how to move her around the floor. Once over his initial qualms, he is stunned by the ease and fluidity and togetherness. 'This publicly permitted parody of an experience he had never had, sexual intercourse, at last liberated his physical response to Nancy.' He asks her to marry him on the spot.

Readers will want to discover the rest of this short and succulent novel for themselves. It's worth saying, though, in point of the woeful neglect of Brigid Brophy's work during the latter years of her life and since her death – a neglect now being redressed by a new generation of admirers – that given our endless interest in matters of sex and gender it is a stunning thing that a writer so uncommonly sharp on these subjects as Brophy should ever have slipped out of currency. Just for instance, had there been a Literary Good Sex Award for grabs in 1962 she would surely have been a nominee, and on account of numerous passages, such as that when she writes of

Marcus and Nancy making love on chill mornings partly to keep warm:

> '. . . instead of pulling up a blanket to cover them they applied to one another. Marcus could plunge himself into Nancy with all the delicious casualness of a man lying on a river bank and lazily inserting his leg in the warm stream, sensitive to, delighted by, the pulsing of the vigorous current against it.'

Brophy is one of a select band of writers who have suffered, most probably, for being too good. As D. J. Enright noted once in the *London Review of Books*, her novels 'have often been described as 'brilliantly written': a judgement which can have done her sales little good. ('Don't bother with that book – it's brilliantly written!') But high prose style – which sometimes, however stupefyingly, gets mistaken for artifice or mere surface polish – is most of the matter in this game. 'True stylishness', says Enright, 'always has a point, and makes it firmly yet discreetly.' Brophy's firmness was well known to those who shepherded her writing into print. As her former agent Giles Gordon wrote in a fond obituary in 1995, 'woe betide the "editor" who tried to rewrite her fastidious, logical, exact prose, change a colon to a semi-colon (or vice versa), or try to spell "show" other than "shew", slavish Shavian that Brophy was'. And 'shew' is very much on display – as is every shining facet of Brophy's gift – in *Flesh*.

Richard T Kelly
Editor, Faber Finds
April 2013

I

MARCUS knew that people must wonder what Nancy saw in him.

Probably they were wondering even while she held her first conversation with him; and when Nancy took him up finally and avowedly, Marcus's sister actually expressed it. "Honestly, Nancy, I don't see what you see in him, an attractive girl like you . . ." It was merely a heavy joke, licensed by the occasion: disparaging sisterly affection towards Marcus, a just compliment to Nancy. Yet it was what everyone wondered.

Marcus wondered himself—but not really in humility. Rather, it gave him a moment's pause of apprehension in the middle of the rapt pleasure he felt because Nancy did see whatever it might be. He was like a derelict property suddenly bought up by a speculator. He was bound to wonder what was to be made of him.

Surprisingly, he did not doubt that there was something to be made. Few people could have imagined he had this confidence. Outwardly, socially, not only was he a hopeless case, but he had obviously written himself off as one. It was quite an ordinary case—of over-sensitivity. The only remarkable thing was the acute degree to which he suffered from it.

His relations with what his parents called other young people consisted in his following, in his empty car, their piled, shouting and erratically-driven cars. In the silence of his car, he lost communication with them, even though he kept their tail lights in view. He could never tell whether they really wanted him to tire, turn off and drive home; or whether they would set him down as more hopeless than ever if he did not presently draw up behind them at whatever house, pub or theatre it was they were being led to by the only one who knew the way.

Yet even in the solitude of his car, he kept the confidence of the over-sensitive: the confidence that he *was* sensitive. So far, it had meant only that he suffered more acutely. When he was invited to parties—at one of which he met Nancy—he diagnosed with hurtful accuracy that he had been asked only on the strategic maxim that good parties needed more men than women. He had had a distressing amount of opportunity to observe, and in perfect detachment, that the strategy worked. It made the women feel that innumerable men were dancing attendance on them, even though some of the men, like Marcus, never spoke (or danced); and the men who did talk to the women, and would have done so in any case, it made to feel that they had fought their way to the women by overcoming rivals. Marcus knew that he was there as a mere extra courtier, brought on to make the production look lavish.

Yet he remained confident that if he was sensitive to suffering he must equally be sensitive to delight—if only the circumstances, by a flick of the wrist, could be turned upside down. Indeed, where it was a question of things which could not be expected to reciprocate his appreciation—books, paintings, flowers, materials—he knew that he did experience a deeper delight than other people. He got more out of them—or put more in; it was the same thing. His delight was intense to the point of agony. He almost suffered it. And by this very token the human relationships which he now suffered could have been turned to delight. His acute sensibility to what other people disparagingly thought of him must be capable of functioning as an acute sensibility to someone's apprecia-

tion. If he was so particularly aware of not communi‹
with most people, he must be capable of precis
minute communication. Only on the question wh‹‹‹‹‹
there ever would be an appreciative person for him to
communicate with did his confidence halt, and he felt
himself depressed for ever on to the side of self-depreciation.

Perhaps what Nancy picked out in him was the
potentiality hidden on the reverse side of his sensibility.
If so, she must have been extraordinarily alive herself to
such potentialities. It would have been hard, the first
time she saw his face, to distinguish anything in it except
suffering.

He had got himself hemmed in by other people's backs
and jammed in a corner between a bookcase and a table
of food, on neither of which was there room for him to
set down his glass, which had been empty for half an
hour. He picked out one of the books, opening up a
black gap on the shelf, and mimed reading. But this
solitary pleasure at a party seemed to him as much a
solecism and a confession as if he had stood there wiggling
a loose tooth in his mouth; and the feeling of being
exposed overwhelmed any pleasure the book might have
given him. He put it back in the shelf, meticulously
aligning it with its neighbours as though it really was a
tooth. He used up as much time as he could. But in the
end there was no more to be done with the books. He
had to turn back to the food table and hover there. His
face might have been a Negro mask attached to the wall,
a great ruby and white badge of over-sensitivity, wearing
a look of Noli Me Tangere.

It was a long, large, terrible face: its size delivered up
every quiver of its suffering magnified, like a drop of
sweat on a face on the cinema screen. On such a scale
the face had room to be both thin and fleshy. Temples,
the ridge of the cheeks, the articulation of the jaw, were

7

all bony. But where there was flesh it was blatantly fleshy, hanging, without shape, on the point of becoming tremulous—or, rather, it always looked as though this was the moment just after it had been flayed, and while it was still quivering.

The lips, especially, were full and almost fruitily suggestive of suffering. They seemed to have been turned too far out, exposing some of the sensitive, private skin that should have been kept inside the mouth.

The nose, when it began, was as narrow and brown as the backbone ridge of a roast turkey; but, by the time it reached the bottom of a curve that really was shaped like a turkey's backbone, it had lost both definition and colour and had become a great blunt truncheon of boneless flesh, which again suggested knives and suffering—suggested, indeed, the ritual surgery of Marcus's race, as though the only way the nose flesh could have been left so tender and exposed was by the removal of a protective foreskin.

He had come to the party wearing a polo-necked sweater with his lounge suit. Even so, no one was deceived into thinking him poor, unconventional or otherwise interesting enough to approach. He emanated the true explanation: that he had sent all his shirts to the laundry at one go and, discovering it too late to buy a new one (he was not in the least short of money), had not known how to ring up his hostess and cry off.

Not that he could think she would have been distressed if he had stayed away. But again he could not tell if it would be acceptable for him simply to fail to come or whether he was bound to offer an explanation, in which case she would have said, "Come in anything" and he would not have known whether she meant it or not.

His face, hung above the food, quivering as if in a faint night breeze, might have been a voodoo talisman warning everyone that the food was forbidden, unclean. But as

8

a matter of fact strategy *had* worked, and the party was going too well for anyone to bother about food yet. Even Marcus ate nothing, though it was not for him the party was going well. It was he, in point of fact, who was troubled by taboo. One of the shallow silver dishes just beside his right hip contained sausage rolls, and he did not know whether the sausages were pork. His host and hostess were Jewish, but not orthodox. The party was mixed Jewish and Gentile: just a party, in fact.

Marcus was not orthodox himself. His parents went to a reformed synagogue, but extremely rarely. They had made no fuss when Marcus stopped going altogether.

Marcus did not, as a matter of fact, like meat in general, because he was squeamish about the killing of animals. Only the pig, through its ancient uncleanness, was too low for his sympathy; and the result was that, by a reversal of the taboo, he actually preferred pork to other meats. As a boy he had had a lust for fried bacon. He had once asked a Gentile friend to ask his mother to serve bacon accidentally on purpose when Marcus was invited to supper. It was wartime, which had admitted dispensations; and those, added to an already liberal background, would have made it perfectly permissible for Marcus to eat the bacon if it could be truly said that there was nothing else and that his refusal would cause embarrassment. But either the friend had forgotten to ask his mother or the family had already eaten up their bacon ration. Marcus remembered they had all eaten a ritually neutral but very unpleasing cheese pie instead.

Now he did not know whether he was more distressed because the sausage rolls might or because they might not contain the only meat he really enjoyed eating.

He did not even feel he could take up one of the paper table napkins which, so many white triangular sails from a watercolour seascape, had been crowded into a smoky Swedish tumbler. It would have relieved him to get rid

9

of his glass, pick out a napkin and fold it into shapes. But the Swedish tumbler had been placed hintingly close to the silver dish: people were obviously meant to wrap a napkin round one end of a sausage roll while they bit the other. Marcus was afraid that a white napkin in his hand might signal to someone to offer him a sausage roll. He would not want his first word to be No. On the other hand he did not want to be seen eating what might be pork, for fear of destroying the last thing he might have in common with about half the people in the room. At the back of many of his motivations was the fear of making himself, if he were not already, unmarriageable.

Yet he could not seriously think he had anything in common with anyone in the room, Jew or Gentile.

As though to mark the very point on which he differed from them all, casting Jew and Gentile alike into the wider class of philistines, he considered plunging back across his tiny corner of space which no one else wanted and looking at another book. His hesitation was acted out bodily. For a moment it was as though the night breeze had produced a gust and the voodoo scarecrow was flapping and spinning.

During that moment Nancy approached him: as though to take him down from the wall or lift him off the stake he was so agonisingly and insecurely impaled on, for ever.

"I knew there must *be* food," she said. "I'm so hungry."

He had no idea it was more than a moment's rescue.

Profusely he offered her, so well as he could with his glass in his hand (but at least it did not have to be kept upright), the cheese biscuits, the canapés, the olives. He did not offer the sausage rolls because he could see she was Jewish. But she seemed, although she had said she was hungry, untempted by any of them. He felt bound to offer her the sausage rolls after all.

"Ah, yes," she said, taking one of the paper napkins,

which he had forgotten to offer, and then one of the rolls. Biting into the roll and looking at Marcus, she said: "It seems so silly to let oneself be restricted by an old hygienic precaution that may have had some point in the ancient world, in the middle east. . . ."

Marcus wanted to say that he believed the theory that it was a hygienic precaution to be a piece of modern middle-class folklore. But he was afraid of sounding supercilious and intellectually aggressive.

"Not that it *is* a hygienic precaution," Nancy went on, on her own account, talking through chews as a gesture of informality, of flirtation even. "It's perfectly obvious to anyone who's read Frazer that it's a straightforward primitive taboo."

Marcus made the motions of gasping—his lips dropped apart—at this revelation that she was an intellectual, too. But no answer would come through his lips, and he closed them again. But, since she had done so, he at least dared to draw out one of the paper table napkins. He rid himself of his glass—there was still no room on the table itself, but he balanced it, carefully, in the silver dish, where Nancy had made a space by taking a sausage roll. He began folding the napkin, again carefully, into shapes, expressing anguish by the violence with which he scored the folds with his thumb-nail, while he waited for the one person in the room with whom he had something in common to walk away from him.

But she did not walk away.

Marcus wanted to dare to ask her whether she liked Proust. Instead, he said, in a depressed voice.

"Do you know many people here?"

"Almost everyone except you."

He gave a giggle, which was really the expression of the gasp which had not come out before. Recovering himself—so far as he was ever in possession of himself—he told her his name, and she replied with hers.

"Do *you* know many people?" she asked.

"Almost no one." His voice did not even pretend that this was unusual with him at parties.

"Presumably you know our host and hostess?" She helped herself to another sausage roll, Marcus's bony hands scurrying to offer her one too late, so that he found himself thrusting the silver dish into her breasts, at a time when both her mouth and hands were already occupied and she could not defend herself against him.

"O yes," he said hastily, putting the dish down, making a sign of apology and blushing, "O yes, I know *them*, of course." And then, fearing he had given an untrue impression and claimed too much intimacy: "But not very well. Actually, she's more a friend of my sister's."

"Is she here tonight?" asked Nancy.

"O yes."

Both Marcus's and Nancy's glance searched the room, hers with purpose, his with none.

"What does she look like?"

"But surely—" Marcus began, before he realised that Nancy had been speaking of his sister, he of their hostess.

In despondency he corrected the misunderstanding. He believed Nancy must think him either witless or insulting to suppose she could have been asking whether their hostess was present at her own party; and he was more pierced by the irony because the whole reason why he had blundered so stupidly was that his thoughts had gone off in pursuit of some sign he might make, some subtle freemasonic code mark he might let fall, that should inform her that he too was intellectual.

Nancy, he learned a year afterwards, had never for a moment taken him for anything else.

"My sister would have been here," he said, painstakingly delivering the full explanation, "only she's gone skiing."

"Do you usually go round with your sister?"

"Yes. I suppose so. Quite a lot. Except when she goes skiing."

Nancy laughed, and Marcus was pleased although he had said it to be truthful, not to be witty.

"I *have* been skiing with her," he scrupulously appended, "but I didn't like it. I mean, I wasn't any good at it."

He had finished folding his paper table napkin and began carefully tearing tiny holes in it.

"Do you live with your sister?"

"No, actually."

"With your parents?"

"No. No, actually, I live on my own."

"What do you do?"

Marcus unfolded the paper napkin and spread it like a gesture of despair. "Nothing," he said.

He knew what effect these confessions, these despairs, of his made on people. He himself was a person who could not look a cripple—let alone in the eye—in the leg; and he knew that his own emotionally, socially, crippled state consisted in his not merely communicating his anguish to others but infecting them with it—so that in all his social transactions both parties had first to blush, then to look away and finally to move away as quickly as social decency allowed, simply through the other people's awareness of *his* awareness of *their* awareness . . . and so on.

But Nancy behaved almost as though she were not a sensitive person. She did not even look down, to where the napkin was stretched between his hands, but went on looking straight at his eyes, which were deep brown, large and—even now, when smoke from the other guests' cigarettes had brought up one or two capillaries in the whites to a cloudy scarlet—beautiful.

"Well, if you did do something, what would it be?"

"O, it would be . . .," he said; and seemed to think for a moment he had expressed himself. "If I were creative," he went on, mumbling, "I'd write a novel."

"What would it be like?"

"Like Proust." As though that went without saying.

"And, as you're not creative——?"

Marcus took curiously kindly to her stating, in this off-hand way, that he was not, instead of assuring him that he might be, that one could never tell, and moving away. He said, almost firmly,

"I'd like to work with beautiful things."

"What type of things?"

"Anything," he said, making peristaltic movements with his hands to urge the completing word through, "beautiful." He added, in a nearly brisk voice, "I might be an art historian."

"Would you like to work in a museum?"

"Yes," he said, "if I could manage the administrative side that is, yes, I'd love to."

His radiance obliged her to say,

"Not that I've got a museum job to offer you."

He looked down again. "No, I know," he said. "And if you had, you wouldn't offer it to me."

Instead of saying she didn't see why not and that he had as good a chance as the next person, Nancy said,

"No, I don't suppose they'd have you. You're not trained, are you?"

"Trained? No."

"What did you do at the university?"

"Actually, I wasn't at the university." He knew he was making it worse, but he added, "I was at a sort of college—well, really a sort of glorified school, but we were all quite grown-up—*in* Oxford. I mean, it wasn't part of . . . But we mixed with the undergraduates quite a lot," he finished, knowing how terrible he sounded— and perhaps was.

"And you like paintings?"

"O, I love them."

"Who's your favourite painter?"

"Rubens," he said.

He knew that Nancy must be seeing the contrast between Rubens and his admirer.

Her eye suddenly descended to the paper table napkin he was still holding open, and she saw he had made not, as she had half-thinkingly assumed when she saw what he was doing, a lace pattern but a silhouette of a kangaroo.

It was his only conjuring trick, and he had invented it himself.

"You're good with your hands," she said, and immediately afterwards looked at the small round gold watch on her small, bare, brown wrist and told him she was going. "No doubt they'll think I only came for the food. And they wouldn't be far wrong. I'm a bit sick of this kind of party. I've met them all—I've met *it*— before."

She smiled and half turned; and he, in an agony to wring from his mind something that should enclose the two of them in a conspiracy against the world, blurted "They're all nothing but materialistic pigs." As she smiled and went, he repeated "Materialistic pigs"; but repetition would not make it either an idiom or a startling metaphor; it was just another of his callownesses.

Yet he felt exhilarated as he drove himself home alone. Even he had not been naïf enough to think she really was offering him a job in a museum: and yet he felt as though he had, for the first time in his life, been canny and worldly, had done himself a bit of good: as though he really had landed a job: or something even better. As he experienced it then, it was the exhilaration of having begun his first business deal rather than his first love affair.

But already he was worrying whether he would be able to bring himself to arrange to meet her again.

2

THAT worry, however, really had been naïf of him. It was obvious from the fact that Nancy knew everyone at the party that they *would* meet again: obviously their milieux were intersecting circles. And as a matter of fact it turned out, when she got home from her ski resort, that Marcus's sister knew Nancy slightly. Nancy had not recognised the relationship from Marcus's surname because his sister was known by her married name. (She was, however, divorced.) When Marcus eventually tried to follow the threads back, he discovered that he and Nancy had just missed meeting a hundred times. Now that each was sensitised to a glimpse of the other, the threads were drawing them towards meeting again—towards meeting increasingly often.

Marcus found this given to him, by society, without his having to bear the embarrassing responsibility of seeking it; and he felt less shy than he would have done because his sister or someone else they both knew was always present, though usually not participating in Marcus's and Nancy's conversation, which was as a rule about the arts. Marcus tried to communicate to Nancy— indeed, he probably did communicate—the agonised, ecstatic rapture that was provoked in him, provoked almost like a rash on his skin, by his sensuous, lyrical response to great blonde areas of Rubens flesh. Nancy heard him quite seriously, penetrating through the callowness of his expression to his thought, and nodding as she gave his thought high marks. But she was not won over to his point of view. At the end she said, "It's no good. I just can't see anything in women of that type." Certainly, it was not her type.

Marcus recognised the distinction that where he was aesthetic Nancy was intelligent. She knew rather than felt about Rubens. But he was not in the least distressed by the difference between them; he was too fully occupied by welcoming the fact that her personality was exactly the complement for want of which his own had limped.

The first time he went out alone with Nancy he scarcely noticed that it was the first time. They both wanted to see the same film. It was rather that they went together than that he took her, though he did as a matter of fact pay, and drove her in his car. On later expeditions, Nancy borrowed her parents' Consul and drove him, because the Consul was more comfortable and better in traffic. It was typical of him, he commented despairingly to her, to have a car which was old but not vintage. "Vintage cars are no good anyway," she said. "They break down if you look at them."

Sometimes he took Nancy back to his flat for coffee after dinner. His flat was in W.1, and the smart address cost him—or, rather, his father—four hundred a year. It was really a single room on the ground floor: there was a squalid cupboard where Marcus had his bed, another, with a rusted geyser, that was the kitchen, and another, without daylight or ventilation, that was the bathroom. In the bathroom the basin and all the ledges were spotted with white smears of toothpaste, which Marcus never saw escaping from the tube and which at first passed unnoticed because they were white on white; they forced themselves on his notice only when they had dried to powder like ointment drying round a sore. He could not find a cloth to clear them up with, and he did not know how to ask the charwoman to do it. When he had insisted on the independence of living alone, he had really made himself dependent on the charwoman. His father had given him a vacuum cleaner with attachments, and he shewed that to the charwoman on her first day; but she said at once, though without specifying them, that she must have other cleaning materials. Marcus had given her two pounds to go out and buy them, but he had never discovered where she kept them.

Even the living room was not really comfortable. Marcus had some pleasingly old armchairs which one could sink into; but in fact, though they were soft enough, one seemed to sink not into comfort but below the surface. The room itself contributed to the impression. It seemed to be half sunk by the bookshelves Marcus had had built along the lower half of one wall. Although the ground floor of the house was in reality raised above the ground level, the room felt as if it were partly let in to the earth. Perhaps it was because all the walls were divided horizontally by a strip of wooden bolection moulding that was just too high: when you sat down, your head came below it; and you felt that you were in a high, square, echoing, indoor swimming-bath and that, weighted down by books, you were on the point of disappearing under water.

Only a few of Marcus's possessions gave him pleasure and pride: his art books, for which he had had a specially deep shelf made—few people he knew possessed both the books and a shelf that would accommodate them; a plain, perfect Chinese bowl of the colour and something of the texture of magnolia petals; a renaissance bronze of John the Baptist, which had been his first purchase in the sale room and which he now recognised to be Victorian—but it was still handsome; a seicento painting which he had picked up for seventy pounds, which shewed a biblical scene by candlelight, and was rather glossy—but although it could not be satisfactorily attributed to anyone it was authentic. He was hampered in his buying by not liking to bid at the sale. He had to leave his bid with one of the officials beforehand. He suspected by this he had sometimes paid more than he need have done; but more often something he really wanted would be lost to him for a mere five pounds he would willingly have given.

As a matter of fact, he knew quite a lot about painting. He had read wide and deep. He had been to the Prado, to Munich, and to Italy five times—though he had not seen all the pictures he ought to have done, because of his unconquerable diffidence about obliging caretakers to open palaces and vergers to open churches. All his visits abroad had been made with his sister, who was older than Marcus and had suddenly, by her divorce, been left companionless just at the time when Marcus was beginning to need her company. She was, in fact, indispensable to his going abroad at all; but within the terms of that, which had to be granted, she was more encumbrance than help. She, who could easily have gotten churches and palaces opened, did not feel interested enough to make the effort. The holiday had to be divided scrupulously between Marcus's interests and hers. She sulked through Florence and Rome, longing only to be off to the Dolomites or Lake Garda; and when it was time to be off, Marcus trailed there despairingly with her and then trailed round despairingly after her, while she, according to season, flirted with ski instructors or exposed herself in a two-piece bathing suit to swimming instructors—none of whom, however, seemed willing to become her second husband.

Marcus's deepest and most private opinion about his sister was that she was really a lesbian. But he was prevented from properly voicing his opinion even to himself by what seemed to him a tacit general belief that Jewish girls never were; the tradition did not make provision for them to be.

He, on the other hand, so abnormal in every other

respect, lacked even the sublimated homosexuality which would have made social cohesion possible; and all his holidays petered out in a series of dreadful afternoons, it hardly mattered whether on a beach or in a mountain hut, when one of these sunburnt, *physical* men whom his sister cultivated would come and lounge beside Marcus and try to chat with him—which turned out to be as impossible as finding a footing in a sandhill or powdery snow. He had finally refused to accompany his sister skiing this winter.

In winter Marcus's flat, though not actually cold, became blackened and frost-bitten. Perhaps the electric bulbs were not strong enough. Often, as the evening settled, he would ring up his parents and invite himself to dinner with them, and then drive out through the dusk to their enormous house near Ken Wood. It seemed hardly smaller than Ken Wood itself; but it was fake Tudor. It had fifteen rooms and a tennis court. Marcus would run his car off the gravelled drive into the laurel bushes, so as to leave room for his father's much larger car to get to the garage. There was always some orange light shewing, through the curtains, at the low, latticed casement windows at the front of the house; and an iron-framed lantern with red, faceted glass hung in the tiled porch. Marcus still had his own latch-key. As he let himself into the hall, he always welcomed the warmth, even though the central heating made an oily smell. But he could not welcome or feel welcomed by the red tiled floor, the oaken settle whose seat lifted to reveal a chest, where no one needed to keep anything, or the discreet door, almost disguised as part of the wall, of the down-stairs lavatory. It was all hideous. It was home, it was meant to make him comfortable, and it was over-furnished: yet it was empty. Everything removed itself, vacated space, asserted nothing—it was too willing to accommodate him.

The whole place was overcast by some relic of the twenties' belief that orange was a jazzy colour. The rooms could be seen only through an orange filter: dilute orange juice on the walls, metallic orange worked into the square light switches, glowing orange in the curtains, russet on the three-piece suite, auburn in the mahogany of the console T.V. Or perhaps here the electric bulbs, behind their square, stitched parchment shades, were too bright. The orange light sought out the emptiness and illuminated the terrible pitch of cleanliness at which Marcus's mother kept all fifteen rooms.

Soon after his key made its noise, a door at the back of the big hall would open and his mother would come to greet him while he was hanging up his coat and scarf. Some of the steam and the smell of boiling would come with her from the kitchen. She had always insisted on doing the cooking herself. She was a big, mumbling hippopotamus figure in an apron, a woman with very little English—with, in fact, no language in common with her son.

When she murmured to him and returned to the kitchen, he would go into the drawing room where, in one of the three pieces, he would find his sister, shewing her nylon knees beneath a tight skirt and reading a magazine. Quite often she knitted as well. She made herself jumpers and woolly caps for skiing.

Here, too, there seemed to him too much polished space. Throughout the house there was too much—parquet, linoleum, sideboards—that *could* be polished; and so long as it could, his mother would. In winter above the smell of the central heating (which made the linoleum smell oily too), and in summer above the scent of the standard roses outside the casements, he was always aware of furniture polish: a smell so dry that after he had inhaled it for half an hour it caused a soreness at the back of his throat.

At a quarter to eight his funny little father came home, and they dined.

After dinner Marcus often felt it was too late and cold for him to go back to his own flat, and so he would stay the night, in the little bedroom his mother kept ready—and of course clean—for him at any time. It was like a bedroom in some hostel for well to do, comfort-loving youth: a plump little divan bed, as neat as something in a ship, covered with a folkweave bedspread; a radiator under the leaded window; a hideous polished wardrobe and dressing table en suite, the dressing table bearing up a triptych of naked looking-glass, the wardrobe gestating in its thigh a set of drawers labelled "Socks", "Studs", "Handkerchiefs". Marcus's sister had a similar bedroom (though he had never discovered whether *her* wardrobe had a space for Studs); and, although this had been her permanent home since her divorce, she had done little to distinguish it from Marcus's or a room in a hostel. She had created nothing except a sub-baroque jumble of cosmetic pots, with costly carved lids which annulled what small pretensions the dressing-table could make to classical bareness; and she had stuck Jean-Paul Belmondo to her wall, on a page torn from a French brown and white illustrated paper.

Through staying the night at his parents', Marcus often was not at his own flat when the charwoman or the laundry man called the next morning, and the result was that his flat became more squalid than ever. He almost gave up trying to live there. Nancy did not like being there, and he took to entertaining her at his parents' house, which was in any case more convenient than dragging her into town. She was living at the moment in Belsize Park, with her parents, though she had at various times lived all round the place.

At first, because she only came to tea, she met only Marcus's sister and mother. His mother gave open signs, even to tears in the eyes, of her joy that Marcus had a girl friend at last. Nancy accepted her joy. Marcus's mother made special cakes for Nancy and at tea would remark, in her bad English, that she had just realised she was still wearing her overall; and she would stand up and remove it. After the first couple of meetings she took to kissing Nancy on the cheek when she entered the house. Nancy accepted that, too.

Marcus's sister, who said she had always liked Nancy, began to make a special friend of her. She took care to stay at home when Nancy was coming, and engaged her in conversations which almost excluded Marcus and in which she shewed more animation than Marcus had ever expected to see provoked in her by someone un-connected with outdoor sports. Marcus even began to wonder if his sister were a touch in love with Nancy.

Marcus's father accepted Nancy as his destined daughter-in-law, and with humble gratitude, even before he had met her. In all matters of taste he deferred to, he indulged, Marcus. He was himself without the ghost of aesthetic awareness. He had not even bad taste: hideous objects came to his possession by magnetism. He had once consulted Marcus about the furnishing of the house, but Marcus had only flinched away from the question, un-bearably impaled on the impossibility of telling the humble comic little man at his elbow that the only thing to do was to burn the place down and start again.

Both parents, although there was not a scrap of his nature in their own, had always allowed for Marcus's sensitivity. He carried all the responsibility of being the son in a Jewish family. They preferred him to their daughter, although they understood her. There was a place reserved in the tradition for Marcus as the un-worldly and dreamy one, and they were quite prepared to keep the place open for him while suffering it to be secularised. Obviously, he was not going to be a rabbi.

But he could be an artist, a scholar, an aesthete, a connoisseur—he could be anything he wanted, with their solemn, traditional blessing and their help. But he did not know what he wanted. And there they could not help.

Nancy, however, evidently believed she could. She rang up Marcus and told him she had heard of a job he could have: perhaps she felt she owed him a job from their first conversation. This prospective job was, in a sense, literary: no money, but it was a way in: it was in advertising.

Marcus declined instantly. He became almost aggressive in explaining that, if he had any literary talent, though he supposed he had not, he would not prostitute it. He was so indignant that he stuttered over the *p* in *prostitute*. Immediately afterwards he felt remorse. He rang Nancy back and arranged to meet her in a teashop in Highgate, where, gazing at her with the passivity of an animal going to ritual slaughter on a frieze, he told her that he would take the job, and would try to do it, if she thought he ought. He put himself in her hands: it was tantamount to a declaration.

Nancy quite accepted the responsibility. But to Marcus's surprise she said that, on thinking it over, she had decided the job was not right for him, and that he should wait for one that was. Marcus had expected her to take the brisk therapeutic line that in a case as bad as his any job was better than no job. Now that she did not, but at the same time did not dismiss him as hopeless, he felt cherished.

When Nancy did at last come to dinner with all Marcus's family, Marcus's father was at pains to amuse her by exploiting his comic personality and even his comic roly, rubbery figure. He spent the evening jumping round her with small servile middle-eastern attentions, bending almost double and bouncing up again. He looked like Monostatos. It would pass, of course, for his wish to make his son's friend welcome; but Marcus knew it was really because Nancy was sexually provocative to him.

It was probably not so much the obvious fact that his family wished him to marry her as the obvious fact that they all—except, presumably, his mother, who in his mind was exempted *ex officio*—found her sexually attractive which persuaded Marcus to welcome her, including her sexual attractiveness, as his own destiny.

3

HE had welcomed it before he properly knew what it
was. At first he hardly knew what Nancy even looked
like. Because of his diffident habit of always gazing down,
he became acquainted with her figure earlier than her
face. It was the figure—small, neat, perhaps more correct
than beautiful—of a wooden dutch doll. And she was
rather the same pretty biscuity colour. Her face was, if
not pretty, comely, and small-featured. She had black
hair, which she wore short and, although it was quite
heavy and thick, kept always neat. The effect of this on
top of her trim, straight little figure reminded one of the
neat black head of a match. She was energetic: brisk and
forthright in movement, yet sharply controlled; she had
the ability to move swiftly and directly to her objective
and then stop dead without noise or untidiness, like a
tropical fish.

She liked organising: liked controlling other people
besides herself. That, fundamentally, Marcus had no
doubt, was why she wanted to marry him. She did not
try to conceal from him that she did. His life had been
spent in an agony of trying to conceal things about
himself—because everything about him was unworthy
of scrutiny—and fearing they shone through. Nancy
concealed nothing. It was almost—not quite almost
insulting, but almost tactless.

Indeed, she had a sort of emotional tactlessness: and
that was her great gift in dealing with Marcus. Socially,
intellectually, even artistically, she could never be tactless.

But in direct personal relationships she had a habit not of failing to see nuances but of naming and discussing them—a sort of coarseness of mind sometimes found in nurses, where it is probably the only way that personalities of a certain kind can practise their profession; but in her it was not a response to circumstance but natural. For Marcus, from whose disabilities so many people had flinched, and whose parents had always made too large allowance for them, putting himself in Nancy's hands was like putting himself, at last, under really competent medical care. To a very, very faint degree, she reminded him of a masseuse.

She was highly intelligent, with a subtle and penetrating mind that was nonetheless not capable of originality. Neither had Marcus discovered any pronounced talent in her. Perhaps she wanted Marcus because she wanted to draw out and form some originality or talent in him. She played the violin competently, but did not have time to practise as she ought. Judging by what she said and had read, Marcus surmised she understood economics; and it turned out that she had at some period done a year at the London School of Economics.

She had, in fact, done a great many things: which was in contrast to him. His curriculum vitae consisted almost wholly of his *not* being called up for the army—he had varicose veins. Besides her year at L.S.E., Nancy had taken a course in domestic science; she had taught the violin in Kent—at a private school for girls, which could not afford to engage a fully-qualified teacher; she had lived for six months with a family in France—and not a Jewish family, either. Her French was excellent. She had had four lovers. Them, too, she did not conceal from Marcus. All her lovers—one of them was the son of the French family—had been Gentiles, and possibly that was why she had not married one of them. At the moment she had neither a job nor a flat of her own; but she had plenty to do; she often translated technical pamphlets for a firm which sold cameras, and she occasionally deputised for the French teacher at a commercial school.

She took Marcus, of course, to her parents' house, which to begin with seemed to him wonderful. On his first visit, both Nancy's parents were out, and he felt free to look at the place scrupulously. The first great relief was that it was underfurnished; and nothing was en suite. The drawing room was occupied simply by a few contemporary-style armchairs which seemed to have been merely left standing about at whatever angle the last occupant had pushed them into when he got up. At Marcus's parents' house, the armchairs were too earth-bound to push. The curtains in Nancy's house were tweed. Even upstairs they did not become floral. Neither did the cushions, which were covered only in rep, in strong, pure colours. The floors were either left to themselves or covered with some sort of coarse, ribbed matting. Books lapsed all over the place, as naturally as uncultivated flowers: some in piles on the floor, besides an armchair, some inclining spaciously in the segments of what was not so much a bookcase as a room divider. *His* parents had had no books in their house since he had moved out. Looking round, he thought that the biggest single difference was that in his parents' house all the rooms had a picture rail, even though no pictures hung from it: here the picture rails had been torn out and the walls whitewashed, and the pictures were nailed straight to the wall.

He told Nancy that he thought the house wonderful.

"I think it's awful," she said.

He commended the absence of picture rail.

"But have you looked at the *pictures*?" she asked.

He had to admit those were awful: he had been trying not to see them. They were without individual personality and yet without the discipline of any style: merely "modern"; not naturalistic, but with some sort of blameless subject, landscape or still life—so incompetently blobbed on that it was hard to tell which. They might or might not all be by the same hand. Most of them had thick bluish-black signatures, strictly illegible but not suggesting a name that was or expected to be known. They were framed in wide, slightly bevelled strips of creamish pebble-dash—and unglazed, of course: indeed, it would have been hard to get a glass on over the high, impassioned but purposeless impasto.

After he had walked round and examined them all, he became aware that they shewed the same predilection for orange as his parents' furnishings.

Even so, he was not immediately disenchanted with the house. It still spoke to him of a freedom of life not to be found at his home: even though, he had to admit, he could not honestly say there was anything he had ever wanted to do and had not been allowed to.

At least in Nancy's home there was neither T.V. set nor radio; only what she called a record-player. In his home it was called the gramophone, was in fact part of the radio and was in any case never used. At Nancy's home *The Radio Times* did not occupy an almost liturgical position—the scripture for the week—at the heart of the drawing room.

Probably her parents were no richer than his. Yet he felt they belonged to a much higher—and freer—social class.

This was confirmed by what she told him about them. Though they had never divorced, they did not get on: "which is presumably why," Nancy said, "I am an only child." They lived separate lives. Indeed, each of the three people occupying the house seemed to do so quite independently. This again appeared to Marcus to denote a freedom. If he rang up Nancy and one of her parents answered, it was never known to them whether she was in or out, or—if, for instance, they knew she was out because she had borrowed one of the cars—when she would be back.

He met the mother first, when she came home unexpectedly early one afternoon to change for something she had to go to that evening. She was in a hurry, of course, her thoughts already in the bath, and she received Marcus's presence with rather preoccupied kindness. Yet it seemed to him that she treated the meeting as important, something she had for some time meant to attend to, though she had not foreseen it would take place on this particular day. Evidently she knew he was going to marry her daughter. He noticed later that she always was rather worried and tired; and that she always wore a shaped felt hat, resembling a fondant, beneath which she shewed precisely four brown sausage curls; he sometimes wondered if hat and curls were part of a single, sub-legal headdress. She really had been a magistrate for a while. Now she did social work and engaged in local Labour politics; she often talked, in a tired voice, about the difficulties of getting East End families to use contraceptives.

The father had nothing in common with her except kindness and perpetual tiredness. But with him the tiredness was more elegant, more yawning. He was a rather elegant man: tall, thin and with a handsome face to which he gave a look of ageing sleekness by wearing a line of moustache that followed the curve of his mouth. This moustache, however, which at first suggested the seducer, still competent if out-of-date, took on quite another and disconcerting, Asiatic character once you realised that his handsome face was in reality quite flat—that he had, like an oriental, no profile. Once noticed, the absence had the power to obsess the noticer: Marcus spent the whole of one evening dodging about to get a side view of him, in pursuit of a profile that had never existed.

On a Sunday afternoon when Marcus and Nancy were playing Bach on the record-player, both her parents—whom they had not known to be in the house—came severally into the room, nodded, sat down and heard the music out Then, after a little tired polite conversation, as much with each other and Nancy as with their guest, they severally departed. Attracted by the music, they seemed to have crept dumbly on stage, sat transfixed till it was over and then pointlessly departed, like the animals in *The Magic Flute*.

Marcus began to conclude that what he had taken for the freedom of Nancy's home was only another version of the emptiness he found in his own.

Marcus had only one more fact to learn about Nancy's father. One mild evening which already shewed signs of spring, he walked along the road with Nancy to buy some extra milk at the half-timbered dairy on the corner; and a neighbour, digging her front garden, called out to Nancy to ask if the Commander's cold was better. Nancy's father *had* had a cold recently; so as soon as they were out of earshot Marcus asked why, if it was her father who was meant, he was called Commander.

"Well, I suppose because he *is* one—or was," Nancy said. Marcus knew him only as a partner in an import and export firm, where he worked very long hours. "He retired after the war. He seems to have spent the war being brave. He won a number of medals. It was desperation, I expect." Marcus never received any other insight into her father's personality, and Nancy did not know any more about it to tell him.

As the year progressed towards spring, his judgment turned definitely against her parents' house. With the windows open to fresh air and stronger natural light, it seemed more open to criticism. One day, when sunshine was falling through the drawing room windows and its warmth was perhaps bringing out the scents of the house, he actually detected the smell which permeated his parents' home. He had already told Nancy that he had come round to her opinion of the house; and now he said:

"D'you know, I think your mother uses the same furniture polish as mine."

"It wouldn't be surprising," Nancy said. "I expect all the retailers in North West London stock the same brands. It's the North West London smell. It stretches as far as Hendon."

She seemed to sniff the air for a minute, and then gazed through the windows into the sunshine.

"When I'm married," she said presently, "I shall never set foot in an N.W. postal district again."

Marcus did not take up the mention of marriage, because his thoughts were still pursuing the scent. Hatred lending him almost inspiration, "I think they must make a kosher furniture polish," he said.

In early spring, one of the girls whom Marcus, his sister and Nancy all knew held a dance. It was being given for her, by her parents, at a roadhouse outside London and was to be a large affair, to which the parental generation was invited, too; and so the two sets of parents met—after the two cars had trailed one another through a rainy night all the way out there; Marcus was driving his father's car and it seemed natural to him to follow Nancy.

They encountered one another, Marcus thought, definitely as the parents of an engaged couple—though, of course, the engagement could not be official, because he had not yet proposed. In a way, he liked testing his acceptability without an official announcement. It gave him great pleasure that people would think of him as a possible, a plausible, and not inherently absurd and to be dismissed out of hand fiancé.

Nancy's mother, hatless for once but her hair still shewing the shape of where the hat had been until an hour before, like a pudding turned out of the mould, was kind to Marcus's mother, now a hippopotamus in navy blue, with openwork sprays of flowers—edged by navy blue sequins—let into the material above the bust. On her it was an overall which seemed to have left its shape after being removed at the last moment. There were smiles but little communication between Nancy's mother and Marcus's, because of Marcus's mother's bad English. The two fathers were also kind to one another; but conversation was impossible between their heights. The four parents stood at the edge of the dance floor, watching the young people—but not their own young people, an awkward little knot because there were three of them—dance. Whenever Marcus's father saw a pretty girl dance by, he nudged the Commander's hip, which was as high as he could reach in comfort; and the Commander, not understanding in the least what his attention was being called to, smiled down, distinguished, withdrawn, kind.

"O God, "Nancy said. She said to Marcus's sister, "Do you mind if I take Marcus away? I can't stand it a moment longer."

"Where can you take him to?"

"To dance."

"Marcus can't dance," his sister said.

"No, I'm afraid I can't," said Marcus.

"That doesn't matter," Nancy said. "I'll teach you."

His first step on the dance floor seemed to him more terrifying than the first yard a car had moved under his hand. That had happened when he was very young and perhaps more robust, and neither had it happened in public. But, he was amazed to find, Nancy did teach him. At first he could not bring himself to obey her instruction not to look down, which was as impossible-seeming as the instruction to take one's feet off the bottom of the swimming bath. But as soon as he did obey, it really was as if he had suddenly discovered how to float.

33

"There, you see," she said. "Providing you don't look at them, my legs will tell yours what to do. It's a sort of physiological telepathy."

They told him more and more complicated things to do; and he followed without a stumble. She danced, as he might have foreseen, excellently.

As they danced past the four parents, Nancy looked at them out of the corner of her eye; and found, of course, that out of the corners of their eye they were watching her and Marcus.

"O God," she said, tilting her head back so as to speak into Marcus's ear, "aren't Jews awful? They're already visualising the grandchildren."

But Marcus was wrapped, enchanted, in his discovery of dancing, which felt to him like floating not in the water but in the air. He did not care who was watching or visualising what. This publicly permitted parody of an experience he had never had, sexual intercourse, at last liberated his physical response to Nancy. He was amazed to find it so unlike—and yet so exactly the realisation of —his erotic daydreams. It was easier; the imagination need not be worked, but responded of its own instant accord to the actuality of the thing—a real person, real legs, moving: yet because of the actuality it was also harder, inasmuch as muscles had actually to grip and let go, air to be displaced. And in the same way it was both less and more exciting.

When the import of Nancy's remark penetrated into his daydream-actuality, he had an urgent sense that he must act at once to make sure the erotic feeling would always be available to him. Diffidently he put it, to the side of Nancy's hair,

"You wouldn't marry me, I suppose, would you?"

"Yes," she said, "I think we ought to get married about May or June." Yet she did not say it in a matter of fact way, but more as though she had been snatched into

34

the same urgent moment as he, and could hardly spare breath for more than telegraphese.

When the music stopped, they rejoined the four parents and Marcus's sister, but they said nothing of their decision.

"You dance awfully well," Marcus's sister said to Nancy. "What was that twiddly bit you were doing, sort of outside Marcus?" She held up her arms for Nancy to partner her and demonstrate it.

Dancing instructors, Marcus commented to himself, must now be added to her list.

But Nancy said:

"Marcus will shew you. I can't bear dancing with women."

So he was obliged to ask his sister for the next dance. He could not, of course, shew her the step. He could barely get round the floor with her. It was not in the least like dancing with Nancy. In the end they stood more or less on one spot and rocked to and fro; and then he confided to his sister that he was engaged to marry Nancy.

Everyone was delighted.

Next morning he telephoned Nancy and took her for a long hard walk across Hampstead Heath. In the middle of the Heath, he confessed to her that he was a virgin.

"Yes, I know you are," Nancy said. "That doesn't matter."

4

EVEN during the engagement, people remarked how much better Marcus was looking. Obviously they were not talking about his health: varicose veins were not a disease. Even so, the improvement evidently shewed bodily. His mother, like some greedy Gentile pigbreeder, poked him in the ribs and said "Fatter". His sister said his face had filled out lately. Perhaps some of his hollows really were filling out, but he himself, when he looked at his reflexion, was aware that the true change was in the cast of his face—in the cast of his figure, even. His flesh was beginning to lose that look of instant, reflex withdrawal from everything, like the automatic shrinkage of amoeba substance from a noxious drop introduced into its microscope slide.

His new well being was like an exposure to the spring sun. It made him sluggish; it almost doped him: but he felt that his impression of exhaustion was really caused by processes of germination in his personality which were using up his energies out of sight. He ceased to anticipate what the world was going to present to him, because he was confident that even if it presented something noxious Nancy would neutralise it. The period of engagement was a raft on which he waited—quite comfortable, actually, quite in the sun—for her to rescue him finally.

He realised that if he had experienced far fewer social agonies than he had expected in meeting and becoming familiar to her parents it was not, as he had at first assumed, because of any particular freedom in their way of life but because Nancy had been steering him without his knowing. He recognised this in arrears because he now became accustomed to her steering touch through the more remote reaches of her family, to whom she had to introduce her fiancé. He always felt a little dread as he drove with her to one of these meetings, but none while it took place. He even felt, after some of them, that he had made quite a good impression.

He was helped by the fact that it did not matter whether he did or not. Nancy called the whole business dreary.

"I expect, if we bothered to look into it, it would turn out that you and I are ninth cousins," she said to him.

Some constellation in his mind, connected with the fact that he had just been watching Nancy and his sister holding a conversation side by side on the sofa, made him reply.

"That's one thing in favour of incest. It would at least economise on meeting the relatives."

Now that he was capable of making quite a good impression, he half wished that some of these meetings *were* important. Or at least he thought he was conscious of Nancy's wishing so.

She steered him not only through his introduction to her relations but through her introduction to his. His, he thought, must have felt it was a new Marcus they were meeting quite as much as an unknown Nancy. He cared nothing for their opinion, of course; yet it gave him a generous pleasure to know that when all these cousins, aunts and paid companions noticed the improvement in him they must, quite correctly, attribute it to Nancy.

It crossed Marcus's mind that, since Nancy had had lovers before, she might allow him to become her lover at once. But she made no move in that direction; so neither, of course, did he.

And as a matter of fact there was no opportunity. They had nowhere except their parents' houses. One of the first things Marcus had done, on their engagement, was to rid himself of the lease of his flat: he had even sold it quite advantageously. He sent his armchairs into store. His books and his objects of art he had crated up professionally and sent to his parents' house, where he did not unpack them. It was quite sensible not to, because they would only have to be moved on again when he and Nancy found somewhere to live. But at the back of his mind he knew that was only a pretext; not to unpack them was a sign of his new sluggishness. He did not feel so much need of his beautiful objects as he had used to—not even of his Chinese bowl. It was as if he did not feel so much need of the agony its beauty caused him.

That, of course, was because a new scale of sensuous experience had come within his range—or, rather, had possessed him, was playing on him, like a rainbow cast on his flesh by a window pane; for he was completely passive towards it. Again, it was part of his feeling of emerging into the sun of an unfolding year; the feeling which kept such step with the fact that the growing spring really was unfolding. He had a half-irritated, half-excited sensation, a prickling in the nostrils and the layers of the skin, as though the air which touched him was a suspension of pollen and the creamy scents of particularly rich flowers—which it really was, of course, as well. He knew this was an erotic sensation. He could tell that by comparing it with the feeling he had had when he danced with Nancy. That feeling, however, he now judged by the fact that it had come to him in the dark, still frosted days of February. It had been brave for the time of year, no doubt, but it was a mere crocus or snowdrop—and as pure. He was aware now of an impatience for fuller-blown experience. He was passive enough, waiting on his raft; but if he had had to wait much longer he would have felt discomfort. He signified his impatience by not eating very much; so that the filling out of his face and ribs, which was now undeniable, must have been effected by a redistribution, not an addition, of weight.

All the same, he had been right when he compared the feeling of dancing with Nancy to an erotic daydream; and that element remained even in his new, further opened feeling. It was a feeling in which she figured—in which *of course* she figured; but in which, rather puzzlingly, she was not central, or did not stand alone in the centre. His prickling excitement was inseparable from an excitement about himself, about his new self. His desire for her was equally capable of attaching itself to his own Ego, which he had for so long disparaged, excused, suffered shame for, and which suddenly didn't need any such thing but could be appreciated and cherished—by himself as well as Nancy. The thin mist of eroticism which now hung over all his days from earliest morning, like the faint hint of an early heat haze, was partly provoked by the fact that his own face, in the morning shaving mirror, was almost good-looking. If he was a spring flower, it must be a narcissus.

They were married on the first of June from Nancy's parents' house. Marcus was twenty-eight, Nancy twenty-nine. All the guests said that the year's seniority did not matter in the least.

The honeymoon was to be in Italy. Marcus had imagined that Nancy might suggest Italy for the tactful reason that he knew both Italy and Italian better than she did and would be in a position to shew her round and take care of her. But of course she was not tactful. She had inclined at first towards France, because she knew it. It was he who persuaded her for Italy, which he was longing for. His sister had been a touch sulky about his refusal, for once, to accompany her skiing, and had hinted that, now he had broken the habit of their holidaying together, she would make difficulties about resuming it. So, if he had not met Nancy, he might never have seen Italy again. He had long before marked down Lucca as the place where he would like to spend his honeymoon, though in those days he did not really expect ever to have a honeymoon.

Laundered, shaved and after-shaved, Marcus looked very well at his wedding. He was, now that he held himself better, quite a well-built man, with quite a handsome face, if you liked—if you could take—fleshy, high-featured, rather Wellingtonian faces.

His sister, whose age also entered the discussion (it was thirty-three), wept when the couple departed.

5

NANCY did have a talent. It was for sexual intercourse.

However, Marcus did not discover this on his first married night, which was spent on the night flight to Milan. He had chosen to take that flight not because it was cheaper but because he felt they must get out of England at once, and he would not consent to a night in France on the way. At Milan they had to spend several cold and colourless dawn hours waiting about in the air terminal before they could catch the train to Lucca. The agent in England had misinformed them about both the time the train left and how long it took. They did not reach Lucca until well after midday, when they were grittily and rather irritably fatigued without having taken enough physical exercise to be tired.

For Marcus fatigue was exacerbated by anxiety, which would not allow him to doze off or even settle into silence. He was terrified of making love to Nancy and also terrified of failing to. He believed his knowledge of the Italian language to be on trial whenever a ticket inspector or coffee-vendor pulled open the door of their compartment. He was afraid the charm of Lucca might not exercise itself on Nancy. He kept jumping up to look for Lucca out of the window long before it could be due, meanwhile explaining to her that it might have changed since he had last been there, that the station was miles from the real town, that she was not to judge the town by the area round the station, which was designed merely for tourists—instead of taxis, for example, there were horse-drawn carriages; and that, since one could do nothing to help them, it was better not to look at the horses as one passed, though as a matter of fact they were probably thin as much through the climate as through ill-treatment.

Nancy did nothing towards calming him. It would have been impossible anyway. She merely sat very still in her corner of the carriage, looking unusually pretty: but that, instead of calming Marcus, worried him, because, he was distressed to find, it did not provoke him in the least.

At the hotel, they decided they did not want luncheon but did want sleep. Marcus left their passports with the clerk at the reception desk and received in exchange another source of worry: Nancy had had, of course, to apply for a new passport in her married name; it had been held in custody by the rabbi and handed to her only after the wedding; and now Marcus could not get it out of his mind that if the clerk noticed that her passport was only one day old the whole staff of the hotel would quickly know that they were newly married and that he was anxious.

He managed to get them and their luggage into the bedroom, though it was Nancy who tipped the porter. Marcus had not forgotten to; it was merely that he failed to see his opportunity. There were two beds, one double, one single. Nancy slipped out of her shoes and lay down on her back, with her ankles crossed, on the single bed. She offered Marcus no caresses; not even an endearment. He lay down, on his side, on the double bed, his cheek in the pillow but his eyes open, watching Nancy. He camouflaged his discontent under a profession of being immensely tired. In his heart he did not believe either of them would sleep. But the afternoon heat had begun, and they both slept soundly, though rather sweatily, till six.

He took her for a walk round the ramparts. Then they had a Cinzano. After strolling about for a while, they had dinner, in the open air, at the restaurant attached to their hotel. A pre-dusk descended as they drank their coffee, and one or two bats came out but stayed far away from the people.

Finishing her coffee, Nancy said:

"Darling, you're scared stiff, aren't you?"

Although he knew it so well, Marcus was astounded by her tactlessness. He was astounded into saying:

"No. No, not at all, not in the least."

She gathered her handbag from the extra chair which the waiter had placed specially for it, and stood up. "Come on."

As stiffly as though he were trying to conceal intoxication, he followed her into the hotel, across the hall, up to the desk. He was ashamed to be asking for their key when it was still not more than nine o'clock, and he stumbled over the number, confusing *sei* with *sette*, a thing he was at all times careful not to do. But the clerk recognised them and gave them the right key in any case. Marcus was ashamed of his mistake and of the clerk's condescension, which seemed to brush aside Marcus's Italian and imply that it would have made no difference if Marcus had not known any. He dreaded the implications in the fact that the clerk had recognised them. As he folded back the gilt grille and ushered Nancy in, he was ashamed of the bedroom farce associations of lifts. As the lift rose, he was ashamed in retrospect of the perfection of the evening, the warmth of the air round their table, the romantic dusk, the latin dinner à deux. . . . It was like something in an illustrated travel brochure. And for him it was a parody of the romantic. He was convinced he would never be able to behave with the vulgar normality of the men illustrated in travel brochures.

But Nancy appealed to his body, and roused it, with

43

a couple of caresses. She had small, swift, soft, brown, cool hands. She also had her—as it was in relation to him—gift of tactlessness. She talked to him. Marcus had always imagined that when he did at last make love to a woman it would be in terrible silence, interrupted only by such noises as their bodies might involuntarily make, which he had already conceived might be embarrassing. But Nancy talked to him about what he was to do, about what he was doing, in a low, rather deep, swift voice which provoked in his skin almost the same sensation as her hands. When he entered her body, he felt he was following her voice.

Where she led him was a strange world that was not new to him, since he had always known it existed, subterraneanly: a grotto, with whose confines and geographical dispositions he at once made himself quite familiar, as with the world of inside his own mouth: but a magic grotto, limitless, infinitely receding and enticing, because every sensation he experienced there carried on its back an endless multiplication of overtones, with the result that the sensation, though more than complete, was never finished, and every experience conducted him to the next; a world where he pleasurably lost himself in a confusion of the senses not in the least malapropos but as appropriate and precise as poetry—a world where one really did see sounds and hear scents, where doves might well have roared and given suck, where perfectly defined, delightful local tactile sensations dissolved into apperceptions of light or darkness, of colour, of thickness, of temperature. . . .

Sensuousness and passion, which his imagination had apprehended to be antithetical, were in Nancy's world plaited into such a perfect interpenetration of opposites that the one could grow as a climax out of the other. Her face would lie for a slow moment above his, her eyes piercing his, until gradually her lips would descend on his full lips, slowly enclosing and enfolding them into a tender intensity of such sensuousness that it comprehended the sensations not only to taste and of texture, but of gentle, exhausting exploration. And yet, even as he felt drained, a climax would gather out of his pebbly dryness like a wave re-forming in its moment of being sucked back, and he would heave himself up, curling above her like a wave, and would snatch, rape, her into an embrace of bitter, muscular, desperate, violence, that could only, he felt, be resolved by a death agony. . . . Yet in reality even this crisis opened, as if on the clash of a pair of cymbals, into a sunlit, flowering landscape, in which one of the flowers proved, subtly, surprisingly, to be his left ear, into which Nancy's finger was inserted— making an effect of wit, to which his response of a sharply indrawn breath made an effect of repartee.

It was a grotto, a private, underground, enchanted folly, of which neither of them could have enough. It became unnecessary for Nancy to guide him into it by talking to him—at least with her voice; he became capable of following the commentary of the very pulsations, the sudden constrictions, the watery unloosenings, of her body's response to the pleasure his body gave her. They made love at night, at dawn, during the siesta—and at half past eleven in the morning, after a certain look exchanged between them, while they were taking a walk on the outskirts of Lucca, had sent them with a single accord racing back to the hotel and up to their room, where the maid was finishing the vacuum cleaning and they stood over her, urging her out, with a silent but nonetheless quite shameless impatience. "Honestly," Marcus said, "if she hadn't gone *then*, if she'd stayed a moment longer, I'd have said she must just take the consequences. Perhaps I'm an exhibitionist as well."

"As well?" Nancy's voice queried, softly, insinuatingly, smilingly curling its way like smoke into the hair on the back of his head, which she was kissing. In bed she had an almost sly, provocative sense of mockery. It was only in mentally defining it that Marcus caught himself recognising that out of bed she had none.

"What do you mean, as well?" she teasingly insisted, whispering.

"Well. . . ." he explained, burying himself deliciously deeper in the bed, and presently deeper in her, as though to answer by demonstration and at the same time hide his blushes, though really he felt no blushes at all; and she sustained his shamelessness by telling him, again in a whisper,

"Nothing is perverse. Nothing at all, if you really want to do it."

They acted on her apophthegm.

But presently Marcus reversed it and whispered, in an appreciative voice,

"Everything is perverse. If you really want to do it."

6

HE had changed, utterly.

Of course it was not the four weeks of honeymoon which had accomplished the change. That was the result of the whole process of knowing Nancy. But the honeymoon made it impossible for him to slide back. It was with incomprehension that he remembered the frame of mind he had brought with him to the hotel, how he had repented ever permitting himself to be rescued at all and wished he had remained for ever hemmed in to a corner where no one expected anything from him because everyone saw him as incapable.

Now he did not care what thoughts the hotel clerk nurtured about him. It was like his not caring what people thought when he was dancing with Nancy. He was prepared to hurry her across the hotel foyer into the lift at no matter what improperly suggestive hour of the day. When he went to wash, if Nancy's dressing gown was nearer than his, he simply thrust himself into it, where his arms protruded a long way further than the sleeves, and swished down the corridor not caring in the least if someone guessed or even glimpsed that beneath its flounced, flowery cotton skirt he was, and very masculinely, naked. Sometimes, if Nancy wanted to sleep in the afternoon, he would lie naked on the bedroom floor in front of the window, sunbathing; and though he had tried to arrange the slats of the venetian blinds in such a way that no one could see in he did not much care if he had failed in that purpose providing he had managed to cut the sunshine down to the temperature he liked.

Once, as he lay there on his back, Nancy crept out of bed, came and lay beside him, but some way apart from him, and, merely by looking intently at him, made his flesh rise. He turned over on to his front not in shame but teasingly, to deny her the satisfaction of reading his confession of her power.

He knew that she had taught him love; just as she had taught him dancing. He knew that he was, now, an excellent, expert lover—at least with her; it did briefly occur to him whether he would fail with another woman, just as he had at dancing. But in any case he quite saw why Nancy had not bothered to persevere with his dancing lessons, when this far more exciting and exacting expertise lay beyond, within her power to teach and his to learn. He thought he knew now what potential talent it was in him which had attracted Nancy to him. She had trained him, of course, to her requirements. He was, in a sense, trained and plumped up for her harem. Yet this thought caused him no smart in his self-esteem. He was quite prepared to strut along beside her, to be her plump little protégé. If the thought did not wound and diminish him, it was because some of his excitement still seemed devoted to cherishing his self. It was her body which provoked his sensations, yet it was his which entertained them and brought them out as on a sounding board —he who was the sensitive instrument.

He felt as though this were a selfishness, a disloyalty even, an impediment in his perfect surrender to Nancy; and so he scrupulously and conscientiously tried to explain it to her.

"Don't you know," she replied, "that one of the things about love is that it enables you to love yourself, too, because it shews you yourself through the other person's eyes?"

He and Nancy always spoke of love, not of being in love.

They planned to go home, without any precise time-table, by way of Vienna and Munich, where the only appointment they had set themselves was that Marcus should convert Nancy to an appreciation of Rubens. But he could not bring himself to break with the spell of Lucca.

"I want to stay here for ever."

"No, you don't," she said. "Eventually, you'd want to do something."

"What?" he asked lazily. "Anyway, I could do something here. Why shouldn't we simply stay? I'd like to live in Italy."

"No you wouldn't. Not after a bit."

"Why not?"

"Well for one thing—the first thing that occurs to me —you'd get sick of never being able to hear any decent music."

"Yes, that's true," he said. "I suppose there could be gramophone records, though. And anyway," he added, rolling over and touching the soft part of her throat with his tongue, "I make music of my own. I play on you." And on myself, he added mentally.

A day or two later she urged him to book their seats for Vienna and Munich.

"Why? Are you longing to go to a concert?" he asked.

"I wouldn't mind, as a matter of fact," she said. "Would you?"

"No, if it would come to me, here."

"I want us to leave Lucca," Nancy said, "before we've exhausted it."

"You're ruthless," he said. "You're an artist in love: I'm just a sensualist. I can't bear to leave *until* I've exhausted it."

"If you're really such a sensualist, I should have thought you'd be raring to get at all your big blonde Rubens women. You know, don't you," she added, "about the man who went round an exhibition of Rubens and came out a vegetarian?"

"I'm the one who went in virtually a vegetarian and came out a carnivore. But actually, I don't want Rubens women, if you don't want to share them."

"I can't share your women," she said.

"Why not? I know you're capable of loving a woman."

"What makes you think so? I'm not, as a matter of fact."

"If you love me, you must see yourself through my eyes."

"O, well, perhaps myself," Nancy said, "mediated through you. But otherwise—it's the one perversion I have no sympathy for. I've nothing against it. I just don't want it going on near me."

"O my prophetic soul, my unfortunate sister," said Marcus.

"Why, is *she* queer?"

"I think," he said, "she's more than a little sweet on you."

"How loathsome," said Nancy. In the silence which she left to appear, Marcus wondered if he had said that, too—for he really had no evidence of his sister's feeling any such thing—to tease Nancy.

As it turned out, they neither exhausted Lucca nor got to see the Rubenses, and it was, in the immediate sense, Marcus's sister who cut them off. About two-thirds of the way through their honeymoon she telegraphed them at their Lucca hotel to say that Marcus's father was seriously ill.

They took the telegram with them into Milan, slapped it down on the counter under the nose of an English-speaking booking clerk and hectored him into giving them seats on a flight home.

When they reached home, they discovered that Marcus's father was in fact dead. He had never been ill. About half past two on a hot afternoon he had parked his car in a side street near his office, climbed out and fallen dead on the pavement.

Nancy told Marcus later that she had known from the moment of seeing the telegram that his father was already dead. Marcus had never suspected it, simply, perhaps, because he had not been able to suspect his sister of doing something so conventional.

Nancy and he went, of course, to stay with his mother and sister in the house near Ken Wood. As a matter of fact they would have had to go there in any case, as they had still not found a home of their own; Nancy had been reconciled to returning briefly to an N.W. address, while they searched for one in S.W.3, 7 or 10.

Marcus learned of his father's death when he telephoned home from the airport—a conversation which he made briefer than it need have been. He kept cutting his mother short and promising to come at once. Only when he had put the receiver down did he realise that there was nothing he could do to bring his father back to life and, therefore, no need to be so urgent. His mother had been implying as much. But he had believed, during the flight, that he must hurry if he was to see his father alive; and the belief survived the news that he was dead. Marcus insisted, though Nancy told him it was unnecessary, on hiring a car to take them straight from the airport home.

During the drive he become disturbed by the thought that he was now hurrying to see his father dead. He was terrified by what he conjectured would be the social awkwardness of being conducted by his mother to an encounter with the body. He could not confide this terror even to Nancy—and again it was a social awkwardness which prevented him, a touch of nearly comic obscenity in the idea of mentioning his father's body without the connotation of his father's personality inside it. He could not ask Nancy where she supposed his father's body had been put: it would have been like asking where she supposed his father's left leg had been put. Any reference to his father as a physical presence had become impossible because it was impossible to decide whether the physical presence was still a *he* or had now turned into an *it*. Marcus did speak of his father to Nancy while they sat in the car, but he spoke of the whole, living man; his death he treated as though it had been a disappearance into the air.

So—when they reached the Ken Wood house—it might have been. The body was not there. As Nancy could probably have told him if he had asked her, it had been taken first to a hospital and thence to an undertaker's.

Marcus was irritated with himself for his terrors in the car, and also because he had promoted in himself more courage to meet them than he now needed.

Perhaps because he had unexpectedly been spared seeing the body, he seemed not to feel the shock of the death. That surprised him; he had been sure he would feel at least the selfish reaction that his own life had been unpleasingly interrupted. He was even more surprised to find developing in himself on his first night home— and here again, perhaps it was because he felt he had been let off lightly—a strong, tugging, almost anguishing current of grief. The feeling swelled in the days that followed. At moments his throat constricted as though to choke down a great plait, a whirlpool of tears. He was remorseful that there had been so small a relationship between him and his father. More bitterly still, he felt —which at times he thought grossly egocentric and at other times a tribute to his knowledge and acceptance of his father's love for him—a tragic regret that his father had not lived to see the completion of the improvement Nancy had wrought in his son.

Nancy and Marcus would have nothing to do with the

ritual mourning. Marcus's mother, half-heartedly borne out by his sister, tried to keep it up, but they fell away the moment the rabbi's eye was removed from them.

To judge by the mumbled answers she made to neighbours and relations who came to sit with her, Marcus's mother believed her husband's death to be yet another aspect of the dreadful parking situation in London.

Because Marcus's father had not been in the care of a doctor, there had to be an inquest. Marcus attended it. It was swift, not quite perfunctory but unritualistic. Marcus was more moved by it than he was by the actual funeral which followed it.

Nancy's father had begun to make the funeral arrangements while Nancy and Marcus were still in Italy. When the funeral itself was over, the surface of the situation in the Ken Wood house improved. Marcus was no longer worried that there might be a wild expression of his mother's grief. But he knew quite well that she must be still agonised; as, indeed, he was himself.

He did not make love to Nancy while they stayed in the Ken Wood house. She asked for no explanations and made him no invitations: but he believed himself obliged to mention it, though simply saying he did not feel he could.

He had to make the arrangements for Probate, and try to discover the value of the estate. His father's share in the business had been left to him. He had to go down to the office, where he had not been since his father had taken him, as a small boy, for a treat—a bare one, Marcus thought now, since the office was a cramped little wood and leather compartment, all paper, cardboard box-files and piercing brass paper clips left lying about—and interview the other partner.

The other partner insisted on taking him through the side streets to see the exact spot where his father had dropped dead.

When Marcus returned and reported that it was beside a parking meter, both he and his sister dared, though not within their mother's hearing, to make the Jewish joke that their father had dropped dead when he saw how much it was going to cost him.

Privately, to Nancy, Marcus improved on that by saying his father must have pulled in just there in pursuit of some girl. Nancy was not pleased by the remark, and he was surprised that she did not understand it to have generated by an attempt on his part to pick out points of sympathy between him and his father.

After he had settled most of the estate, though he had still not discovered how best to dispose of what was now his interest in the business, his mother told him that he was looking tired. His sister, taking perhaps a feminist line against this Jewish solicitude for the son—or perhaps simply taking a pro-Nancy line—added that Nancy was evidently suffering from the strain, too. Marcus almost credited her with guessing that he had not made love to Nancy since they had come home. So he and Nancy went away for a weekend to an hotel in the country. Although it was, in its Englishness, only a travesty of an Italian hotel, hotels were home ground for their married life, and after dinner they hurried upstairs with a sense of resuming their honeymoon. But Marcus was impotent.

He was furious with himself. His rage was comically— if he had been prepared to find anything comic in the subject—a contrast to the despair and self-depreciation with which he had been ready to accept failure on the first night of their marriage. Now he was behaving like a champion athlete who had unaccountably proved out of form. He made no apology to Nancy; he seemed to think it was only he who had been deprived. He segregated himself strictly in his half of the bed, and went sulkily to sleep.

Next morning he sulked round their bedroom in his dressing gown, looking more than ever like a rich, famous boxer who had been unexpectedly beaten. At eleven o'clock, when the importunate chambermaids could be put off no longer, Marcus grudgingly got dressed, but he went no further than the hotel lounge and, when it opened, the bar, and sulked there.

By evening, drink and staying indoors had given him a headache, and he went early to bed—making it clear, however, that he was too proud to think of trying to make love again.

Nancy was irritated into saying, as she undressed, "You are an idiot, darling. And anyway, anyone with half an eye could see what's at the root of it."

"At the root of what?" said Marcus, choosing at the last moment to pretend it was something else he was sulking about. He was already in the bed, turned on his side, facing away from where she would presently join him. He weakened his pretence by too much fluency of invention when he added, "You mean at the root of my headache?"

"No," Nancy said, getting into bed. "I mean last night."

"Well I must lack even half an eye, because I don't see."

"Don't you even know the curse of your own race?" she said. "Filial guilt."

"If you mean I feel some sort of guilt about my father, you're wrong. I don't feel guilty in the least."

"One doesn't feel things that are unconscious. That's what the word means."

"O well, if you mean I feel something I can't feel, then you're safe in attributing anything you like to me. No one can check up on you. But actually it doesn't seem very likely. Why *should* I feel guilt, conscious or unconscious? I haven't done anything to make me feel guilt."

"Where do you suppose you were at the moment your father died?"

"I was in Lucca, of course. So were you."

"Yes, so was I," Nancy repeated. "And the chances are, you were inside me."

Marcus turned over and faced her.

"If you imagine that's been bothering me, you're wrong again. I've never given it a thought."

"But you don't suppose your unconscious is incapable of making such a simple calculation?"

Marcus looked at her in silence for a moment, from the pillow. Then:

"Sigmunda Freud," he said.

"Well, at least he was a Jew," said Nancy.

Marcus could see no point in the remark, and he turned over and went to sleep.

He woke very early—perhaps as early as five—next morning and, instantly lucid, said to Nancy:

"When you said at least Freud was Jew, did you mean these guilt feelings only apply to Jews?"

He saw she had to make an effort to come out of her sleep in order to receive his question at all.

"No, of course not," she answered presently. "Even you can't be ignorant enough to think Oedipus was a Jew."

"I'd forgotten Oedipus."

"You had," she agreed, and began to go to sleep again.

"What *did* you mean, then?"

"I can't remember. I suppose I meant it's more acute in Jews. Phenomena like that are easiest to study in the most extreme cases. It helps to illuminate the milder ones."

This time she did go back to sleep. Marcus talked on even though he had observed that her consciousness was leaving him behind. "I don't say you're wrong about me. I just say I can't discover a trace of evidence for it in myself. It just doesn't convince me."

Then he went back to sleep, too.

They woke again, simultaneously, at eight. Whether

the explanation she had given him was correct or whether he was so suggestible and so much in her power that he accepted it on her authority he did not know; but she had cured him. He demonstrated his cure before they got up. "That's twice you've rescued me," he said to her, affectionately.

7

It seemed to Marcus that a number of important actions were begging to be done at the same time: either they were begging or Nancy was expecting him to do them. He had to dispose of the business; to find himself a job; to search S.W.3, 7 and 10 for a flat for himself and Nancy; and to make love to Nancy.

Only the last really engaged his interest, though the question of finding a flat did so slightly, because it was connected with making love. After the weekend in the country Marcus found he could make love to Nancy in the Ken Wood house; but they could not enjoy the devil-may-care feeling they had cultivated, now that they were in a borrowed bedroom in a house that was still faintly tainted by bereavement and was in any case a family house: the very fakeness of its beams enjoined the pretence that sex did not exist which had been kept up while Marcus and his sister had been children there. Marcus was therefore willing and even active in driving round the estate agents with Nancy, collecting orders to view.

Another result of the weekend in the country was that Marcus's grief had withdrawn. He tried sometimes to sting it back; and when he failed he tried to lacerate himself by accusations that he was growing unfeeling and had lost his capacity for anguish. But he could not really stir anything. Even when he put it to himself that his grief had become impotent, he was not bitten, but only slightly pleased by his irony.

Eventually one of the estate agents sent them to a flat in Chelsea which was held, on a long lease, by a rich young

Jewish couple who, since buying it, had had four children and now needed a house. Marcus could see that Nancy was displeased by the fact that they were Jews. But even she liked the flat. She admitted, outside in the car, after the interview, that she wanted it. It looked, however, as though the choice was not hers. By the time Marcus and Nancy arrived, the couple had already received an offer; so they merely promised to let Marcus know if the sale fell through.

When he and Nancy got back to the Ken Wood house, Marcus put it to his mother and sister that they no longer needed fifteen rooms and a tennis court, which were only a responsibility to keep up. Both of them agreed. Marcus telephoned the couple in Chelsea and offered to swop the house for their flat.

When they came to look at the house, they were plainly cast down by the thought of accepting it in place of their flat, which was beautiful. But they were won over: by the easiness of selling and buying at the same time, which removed the worry of having nowhere to go and meant they need realise a smaller amount of capital than they had expected, since they need put down only the difference between the two prices; by the usefulness of the tennis court for keeping four children entertained; and, Marcus thought, by a twitch on an atavistic cord drawing them back to North London.

What Marcus had in mind was to settle his mother and sister in a flat in or near Hampstead, the part of the world they were used to. But his sister suddenly wanted to get out of that part of the world. The mother had no preferences: she rarely went out of doors in any case. Since they were neither poor nor particular, it should not be hard to find something for them. Nancy did most of the looking, because she wanted to keep control. She concentrated on W.8. They did not want to be too far from Chelsea and she did not want them to be too near.

She quickly discovered an empty flat in a street off the south side of High Street, Kensington. It had big, high, yellowing rooms, which would accommodate a good deal of the furniture from the Ken Wood house, and was three floors up in a mansion block of crimson brick with cream stone dressings. There was a porter, whose uniform matched the brick, a hall tiled to resemble mosaic, and a 1910-ish lift which appeared to be, though it was not really, worked by the manual effort of heaving on the crimson cord which was threaded through one side. The name of the block was outlandish but unmemorable and presumably borrowed from some overseas victory; the name was worked into a terracotta plate over the porch and woven or dyed into the doormat at the main door, in both cases in a script so wiltingly art nouveau as to be illegible.

Marcus found himself with even more, and even more complex, business to do. It was not very hard to arrange his mother's tenancy of the Kensington flat, which was on only a seven-year lease, and the previous leaseholders wanted the small premium handed over in cash. But the purchase of the sixty-nine-year lease in Chelsea and the sale of the house, which would entail a readjustment of the death duties on his father's estate, took time. He was irritated to find that title deeds had to be searched and leases engrossed even though he and the Chelsea couple were quite willing to believe in one another's honesty. He had imagined it could all be accomplished, as in some dignified primitive community, by the exchange of a solemn word. He had imagined himself making love to Nancy on the bare floorboards of their new home that very night.

Instead, they had all four to stay on in the Ken Wood house half packed to go, through several miserable weeks during which even the summer failed them and turned cold and rainy. Nancy began to talk about finding Marcus a job.

Every evening, while the mother cooked dinner, the three younger people sat in the drawing room, where it was sometimes necessary to light a fire; and every evening it seemed that the conversation was about Marcus's job.

One evening, when Nancy came into the room, where Marcus was already sitting with his sister, he said:

"Here comes the careers mistress."

Nancy did not know how to take the remark.

The next evening, he thought of something that would tease her further still. He suggested that, instead of selling the partnership in his father's business, he should take it up: that would be his job.

"O don't be silly," Nancy said. "You can't be a business man."

"I don't know whether you mean business is unworthy of me or I'm unworthy of business."

"Both—neither," Nancy said. "It's mutual incompatibility. One's only got to look at you to see you couldn't be a dried fruit importer."

"It's just a question of what I should be instead."

"The first time I ever met you, you said you wanted to work with something beautiful."

"Well," he said, pretending to consider, "prunes, raisins—they have a resemblance, you know, to certain faces of Rembrandt."

"You're a Rubens man, not a Rembrandt man," Nancy said, but fiercely, not with amusement.

"I think Marcus ought to do something with his hands," his sister said. "Marcus is good with his hands." She herself was knitting away. Perhaps being good with their hands ran in their family.

"I *know* he's good with his hands," said Nancy, as though jealously; and her tone made Marcus wonder if she had invested his dexterity with a sexual connotation. "But he can't make a career out of tearing paper kangaroos."

61

"Toys, perhaps," Marcus murmured mildly. "Or Christmas decorations—in Australia, perhaps. No doubt there's a market."

"You don't want a market," Nancy replied. "You talk as though we were all still living in the bazaar."

"Life," said Marcus, pretending to give an affected sigh, "is one enormous bazaar." But it didn't amuse Nancy.

In the end, since he *had* been only teasing, he sold the partnership; and at about the same time they at last moved into their Chelsea flat.

His mother and sister were already living in Kensington. It seemed to Marcus that his mother really had taken to a different furniture polish, but it was hard to be sure, because she overlaid the newness of her new flat with the same old smell—or, really, sense—of things being steamed, by relays, in the kitchen. His sister had without difficulty reorientated herself—re-routed her daily steps —from John Barnes to John Barker.

8

IT astonished Nancy and Marcus that moving in could cause them such—and so many days'—confusion, and that it could yet turn out, when the confusion began to lift, that they had virtually no possessions. Marcus's vision of making love on bare floorboards came almost true. In point of fact, they *had* bought a bed. They also had the armchairs from Marcus's old flat; but they sorted ill with the new flat, and were marked down to be replaced. Nancy and Marcus had declined to take anything from the Ken Wood house, even to tide them over. That left them with Nancy's gramophone records and Marcus's books and objects of art.

When he eventually unpacked his objects, he found them faded and diminished by their period inside the crates. And they, too, did not go with the flat; it was too beautiful for them.

Nancy had spent all her days there before the move, supervising its decoration—which really consisted of de-decorating it. They ripped off all the fashionably up-to-date wallpaper the other people had hung—or, at least, they employed workmen to do it, and expressed their own anger at the desecration of the walls by the energy of the instructions they gave. Nancy had almost to bully the workmen, who kept pointing out that the wallpaper was still in excellent condition and had cost a great deal. Then she had to exert her will again to get the place painted a genuine, matt white instead of the glossy cream the workmen said was more practical.

The result was that they themselves, who had picked out and revealed its beauty, were more than ever under a moral obligation not to desecrate the place. There was not a wall Marcus would besmirch with his seicento picture—which had, indeed, just the glossy paint surface they had driven out of their temple. The place *was*, like all eighteenth-century building, a temple: a small and chaste one, where no blood sacrifice had ever been performed. The niche between the long, mannered, exquisite windows in the drawing room (the flat consisted of the first floor of the house) would, Marcus thought, shudder down or fold its wings and brick itself in, if he were to stand his renaissance-Victorian statuette in it.

The place was, simply, architecture; and the problem, how to live in without obscuring it. Both Marcus and Nancy knew how to answer the problem, but they knew it would take time. They could see in their minds' eye the pieces of furniture—very few in number—which they must acquire; not necessarily rare things, but difficult to find, because the just right always was difficult to find.

So, for the time being, they lived in and off scrubbed wood furniture, which pleased them because it announced that it was to be replaced, asserting a mere x or y until the just right quantity should be known.

Only Marcus's Chinese bowl looked at all well in its new surroundings. But, strictly speaking, there was nowhere to *put* even that.

He was trying it out in various places when Nancy came home, after a teaparty he had excused himself from, and disclosed that she had heard of a job she thought he could have if he wanted it.

He instantly armed himself against the idea. "We're not even properly settled in yet. There's no hurry."

Surprisingly, Nancy let the subject drop.

He thought she must be practising the childish

stratagem of making him interested by pretending she was not.

But by the next day he had decided that that was so uncharacteristic of her as to be impossible. So he asked her what the job was.

"I don't think it's for you," she said. "It's in a sort of antique shop."

"How very apropos," said Marcus. "I might pick up some pieces."

"You might pick up other things as well."

"Such as?"

"O, I don't know. Nasty attitudes."

"That," said Marcus, "is the most untypical remark I've ever heard you make." He put down the Chinese bowl so as to turn and look at her face to face.

"How so?"

"Well, it's like saying *bad habits* when you mean masturbation. And one of your immense virtues is that you never do cloak your thought in the decent obscurity of a middle-class vagueness."

"I have to be vague when I don't really know what I mean myself. I suppose I'm afraid you might pick up commercialism. Or dilettantism."

"Well at least not both," he said. "Aren't they contradictory?"

"No," she said. "Not when the commerce consists of selling things to dilettanti."

"Well, at least tell me about the job."

"Darling, it isn't even worth telling you. It's not your sort of job."

"Then tell me just as gossip."

"Well," she said. Evidently she didn't want even to put words to the images. It was with a hasty distaste that she brought out, "Well, you remember that girl Julia——She was at that dance——?"

"Vaguely."

"Well, she has—she's always had—a person, a sort of attachment, whom she calls Uncle Polydore. That's his surname. I don't know whether he's really her uncle or not. I've met him. He's a sort of butterfly—but *old*, you know. I suppose he's queer, insofar as he's anything. Anyway, he has this shop in Wigmore Street. Very expensive. I think he does whole decorative schemes, as he no doubt calls them, for fashionable people. Anyway. Well, anyway, he buys pieces and tarts them up. I daresay he fakes them. Anyway, he's looking for someone with an eye, someone with taste or fake taste, to supervise his restoration work."

"Well," said Marcus. "You've always said I was good with my hands." He looked at them for a moment and then plunged them inside the Chinese bowl, where he made a gesture as though he were using the bowl to knead pastry—or perhaps for some sort of ritual ablution.

9

"DON'T forget they've made Baker Street one way," said Nancy.

"I hadn't forgotten. I know all the routes to North London. I'm a Jew."

"Well, if you want to reach Wigmore Street——"

"I know how to reach Wigmore Street," he said, turning the car into it. "And I know it's I who want to reach Wigmore Street, and you who don't. We'll have to park in Harley Street or one of those."

All the same, she had insisted on coming with him.

"On the contrary," she said while he parked, "I'm glad you're coming, because then you'll see straight-away it's not for you. I only object to the waste of time."

"It's not as if I had a great deal to do with my time. In fact, I thought it was *that* you objected to."

He was ready to get out, but she insisted on sitting still in the halted car.

"I don't *object* to anything, darling," she said, "not to anything connected with you. I'd only object if you made yourself unhappy. Or disappointed."

"Well, I won't."

"I want you to have the sort of job you deserve."

"O well," he said. "You've taken me up. I suppose you're entitled to make something of me."

"Marcus."

"Mm."

"Marcus, don't make me out a bullying female."

He wondered for a moment whether she really meant *make me out*—or *make me*.

67

"Then let's go and see Uncle Polydore," he said amicably.

They got out of the car, and Marcus put some money into the parking meter beside it.

"I hope these machines aren't invariably fatal to my family," he said.

IO

FROM the far side of the street it appeared that two women in evening dress were reclining, impeccably counterbalanced, one in each side of the double shop front. From half way across the road they clarified and angularised themselves into two silk-covered, imprecisely late-eighteenth-century chaises longues, one of which had gold tasselling hung about its shoulder—the sort of parody of military braiding which a woman might wear at a ball where the dances were to be Highland.

The door between them was set back, surmounted by the name S. POLYDORE and surrounded by smooth, newly-washed slabs of a black and dark grey marbled substance which probably was really glass.

It was very posh indeed.

Although the two chaises longues were the only objects actually in the window, where they were raised on shallow, felt-covered platforms, one could see beyond them to the interior of the shop. The prime impression made by the objects inside was that not a speck of dust had been allowed even to float near them; the next that almost all of them consisted of marble supports and gilt sphinxes being supported, interspersed with a few abbreviated runs of leather-and-gilt eighteenth-century volumes. What the eye finally took in was that the clutter of objects, though carefully informal, had been carefully arranged to lead the eye, and no doubt the feet, into the shop, which was rather narrow but deep—like a stage, in fact. There were, though there did not appear to be, two aisles, which conducted visitors through the objects and insisted that they explore the recession of the shop plane by plane—as though they were walking through a picture by Poussin.

The door liberated a short, pretty *ping* when it was opened.

Nancy and Marcus took the left-hand aisle and discovered it had conducted them to—about two-thirds of the way down the shop—a thin, rather good-looking young English gentlewoman who, wearing a short straight skirt and a twin set, was sitting, with her long, very thin legs crossed, behind a pretty little walnut desk. The writing surface of the desk was covered with leather but above that rose a narrow walnut rampart, edged with a tiny brass rail. From most angles the young woman would have been hidden if she had been sitting properly up to the desk, instead of turned sideways, to accommodate her thin knees, which shewed white even through her stockings.

She rose, made a sketch of pulling her skirt down—it would not really come—and asked if she could help Nancy and Marcus.

They explained their appointment.

"Oh yes. Would you mind waiting here, and I'll go and tell Mr. Polydore."

A sort of courtesy, an embarrassment almost, induced by the glossy condition of the objects—and by the inveterate, inculcated in childhood fear of knocking one of them over—prevented Nancy and Marcus from really observing where the young woman went to at the back of the shop, though they were aware that a door had moved, somewhere in the shop's deepest plane.

Marcus fixed his attention, instead, on the desk that had been vacated. He had an impression Nancy was looking round the place, but without moving.

At one side of the rampart of the desk stood a bright brass lamp in the shape of a snake. In place of a shade it had been fitted with a small glass lustre. On the writing surface were two piles of large, deckle-edged visiting cards, on which the young woman had been working with a ball-point pen. The two piles were those she had done and those she had yet to do—though *done* and *to do*, as the piles themselves announced by being on the point of sliding into fans, were desultory terms. Each card was engraved "s. POLYDORE. Objets d'art" and had the address in the bottom left-hand corner. The young woman had been going through them, inking out the telephone number and writing in a new one.

Presently Marcus realised that there arose from the desk a slight smell of the furniture polish which had been used in the Ken Wood house.

Then the door at the back moved again, and S. Polydore came to them.

"My dears," he said.

He was a short little man with a big head, the head made even bigger by a great cowl of brilliantly white hair, the hair made even more brilliantly white by the deep brown of his face—a brown which looked as though he had acquired it from an induced chemical reaction rather than the sun. His big eyes were blue, but blue of the kind which might have had white mixed with it. There was not a wrinkle on his colossal forehead; but his cheeks had fallen in. He must be sixty. In rather the same way, the lower half of his body had fallen in. He was quite plump —or, more probably, plumped out, since it seemed to be his clothes that bulged rather than his chest—down to the middle; but his legs appeared to have wasted, and his putty-coloured cotton trousers, though fashionably and youthfully narrow, hung quite absurdly, as though empty. Presumably, though, he *had* legs, since there were feet at the bottom of his trousers—rather long feet, too; they were wearing lavender suède shoes. Somewhere near his neck, but overshadowed by his big face, was the soft collar of a grey flannel shirt with a scarlet bow tie partly buried under it. He was wearing a fawn cardigan, which had a zip but hung open, and which had blundered into some cigarette ash half way down. In his left hand was one-third of a small, cheap cigarette, whose paper had turned dark brown along one side; on his right, which he held out to Nancy and Marcus, was a gold signet ring.

The preponderance of chest over legs and the sense that the chest was puffed out rather than substantial made him look like a sparrow; and he moved in little fluttering spurts, suggesting that at the end he was going to take off, instead of which he settled into himself, giving off a tiny dusting of talcum powder. Perhaps his fluttering and subsiding had been induced by living among objects he must take care not to knock over.

To Nancy he said, "We must have met", to Marcus, "We haven't." To Nancy again, "At some awful, Semitic *do*." Then, back to Marcus, "You're probably better at getting out of such things than I am." Then finally, to them both, "But how sweet of you to come *here*! I hope this doesn't count as a Semitic *do*."

The young woman, who must have followed him through the door, tried to return unobtrusively to her desk, politely making it clear she was not asking to be included in the group. But Polydore, with one of his flutters, included her, meanwhile asking Nancy and Marcus, "Have you met my window dressing?" To Nancy alone, to whose disapprobation of the whole business he was obviously quite alive, he made a swift aside—"Yes, dear, I did say dress*ing* not dress*er*"—before making, to them both, the introduction: "Miss Theodora Watts-Dunton."

Could her name be Miss Theodora Watts-Dunton, Marcus wondered: it *must* be a mishearing by his over-literary mind: and meanwhile Pollydore was continuing:

"Absolutely genuine one hundred per cent non-Semitic, and genuine débutante. She's been genuinely presented. I mean"—he spread his hands—"the only genuine article in the shop."

Nancy gave the most skeletal of smiles, to mark her repudiation of the impoliteness to Miss Theodora Watts-Dunton, but everyone else laughed—Miss Theodora-Dunton loudest of all. She leaned across and with one of her long, thin, manicured à merveille fingernails flicked one of the lights of the lustre on the desk, and it briefly added its laughter to hers. Neither sound was particularly pretty. "I've *told* you," she said, "you *must* drop the line about me being presented. Now they've stopped presentations, it dates me."

"But, my dear," Polydore objected, horrendously stretching all his fingers like Struwwelpeter, "I shall lose half the effect of class if I do. Besides, nothing in this establishment has a precise date." Waiting for no counter-objection, he went immediately on to hunch his shoulders, thereby drawing Marcus into a huddle with him, where he confided, "And the beauty of it is—I pay her practically nothing. She just likes working with beautiful things."

Again, it was Theodora Watts-Dunton—if she *was* Theodora Watts-Dunton—who laughed loudest.

Marcus thought that a pulse beat in unison between him and Nancy at the phrase about liking to work with beautiful things.

"So do I," he said thoughtfully to Polydore. "But *I*'d have to be paid."

"Ah well," said Polydore. "One can't have everything. Though my livelihood depends on people thinking they can." He stopped fluttering for a moment, in order to consider Marcus carefully, face to face, which meant for Polydore in an upward direction; and Marcus not un-complacently stared candidly back into Polydore's eyes, in which he found he could not really look at the pupil or iris but was led aside to consider the extraordinary yellowness, the nicotine colour, of the whites.

"I don't think, you know," said Polydore, "I'd put you in my shop front. You're not as decorative as Miss Scott-Marmion" (or whatever the name—Marcus knew he had still not caught it—really was). "I think I'd keep you out of sight downstairs."

"Well, hadn't you better shew me the shades of the prison house," Marcus said rather awkwardly, "to see if I take to them?"

He could tell, as he stood back for her to follow Polydore first, that Nancy was resisting his liking for the place and the man. She would have preferred to walk behind Marcus, as though that would have given her greater control.

The whole party paused before going through the door at the depth of the shop and turned back for an instant while Nancy and Marcus exchanged a mimed gasp and a smiling nod, meant to indicate temporary leave-taking, with Miss Scott-Marmion, who was preparing to sit down to her cards again.

They did not much notice the dark tucked-away little rooms or offices Polydore led them through: it was a brief, unrealised little journey, anyway, and they were quickly on the verge of a dark steep drop of stone steps. "*Do* take care—I'll go first—O dear, I do hope you're not wearing *too* high heels—there *is* a sort of cord at the side, if you can find it in this light, but I shouldn't place any sort of *reliance* on it—it makes you feel" (Polydore almost stumbled himself) "there must be a Minotaur waiting at the bottom."

Instead of which there was—a sort of enchanted lumber-room, Marcus thought, as he stood at the bottom of the stairs looking it over and wishing he had had it as a place to play in when he was a child. It was a great, informal stone cavern. It must extend, he realised, under the pavement, perhaps under the street, in front of the shop; and it was crammed with battered old bits of furniture.

74

Broken-winged cupids, tables elegant in line but lacking a leg, amputated chairs: they made it into a derelicts' hospital, but without connotations of suffering—more like a collection of old woollen toys, their disfigurements made endearing by the fact they had always been known and were accepted like the deficiencies of one's own face. Here and there clay-coloured dust sheets had been thrown over some objects, but without enough enthusiasm to get them properly on. An oblong gilt mirror, upended, had lost half its glass, which had prompted someone to shroud it, as though brokenness made it indecent like a naked dummy in a clothes shop; but the shroud was slipping off, listing like candlegrease and dripping onto the floor, where it had already received dusty shoe-prints.

At the far end of the cavern two tall dignified men in dark grey woven overalls were silently shifting some of the furniture about, with the appearance of carrying a sedan chair—or even a bier, in some world where death did not bring sadness.

The place was lit by two long sodium strips on the ceiling, one of which shone directly and blanchingly down on a Chinese carpet, which was in any case white, though with a few figures as sparingly inserted as words in a Chinese poem, and which was draped over the back of a mahogany bookcase lacking shelves. Marcus knew at once, and sensed that Nancy did, that they wanted the carpet for their drawing room.

Because the floor was only stone or because the objects had so obviously been knocked into already, Marcus lost his fear of moving round. He squeezed his way between pieces, touching here, peering under the corner of dust sheets there; and Polydore, himself a trifle less nervous in movement down here, followed him round, like a dwarf displaying his treasury.

"I've gone out," said Polydore, suddenly holding up the tarry stump of cigarette in his hand. "Must be that dreadful draught on the stairs. Where———" He began searching the pocket of his trousers, which, even when pulled taut, still did not suggest there was anything inside. "—I'm so sorry, how dreadful of me, will you———" Evidently, he kept his cigarettes in the breast pocket of his flannel shirt. Nancy and Marcus declined while he was still flapping his hand at the pocket to get them, so he went back to the pocket in his trousers, fetched out his matches and re-lit the remaining inch of his own cigarette, which was as difficult to get going as a pipe.

"I've made a 'no smoking' rule down here. Which is why I compromise by only smoking tiny ones. The workmen think it's so *working-class* of me. But, really, it's *too* dangerous. I mean"—he shrugged—"one spark, and my entire capital would go up. Such as it is. I'm insured, of course," he added, and used his thumb and middle finger to take the cigarette out of his mouth while he began to tug at a dust sheet. "Now here———"

There could hardly be two puffs left in the cigarette, and in any case the dust sheet required both hands, so Polydore threw the cigarette behind him, on to the stone floor. With Marcus's help, he raised the dust sheet and bundled it aside, revealing the wreck of an eighteenth-century French chest of drawers—one of those with bulges near the bottom, looking as though breeches were slipping down and almost off its legs. It had lost its shine; a good deal of the surface had gone milky white, and it was pitted in several places. "You see, what we've got to do is make good the veneer—here, for example, and here—fill in the bits of this marquetry that have come away, bring up the surface, and find something to replace these metal facings."

One of the dignified men in overalls passed silently behind them and trod out Polydore's cigarette as he went.

"Of course, I could have the pattern copied, to fill in the gaps," said Polydore. "But it always looks glaring,

76

you know. Or I could get something made. There's a place out at Fulham that does my metalwork. But you know what they are. They're not artists, they're artisans. They're literal-minded. They do exactly what I tell them. And that's no good. What I want them to do is improvise on a theme I give them. Now here, I thought—something foliated, or perhaps something with scrolls, or even sea-shells. But it's no good telling them that. The trouble is, I can't visualise. I can buy. I can sell. But I can't visualise."

Marcus took his diary out of his pocket and stood for a while looking at the chest of drawers. Then, on a blank page from earlier in the year, he drew—or, rather, made a diagram of—a complicated little rococo frieze, and shewed it to Polydore.

Polydore looked at it as it were in despair, then at the chest of drawers; and at last he transferred his despair directly to Marcus. "I wish I could do without you," he said.

"Maybe you can," said Marcus. "Think about it." He put his diary away.

"I don't need to," said Polydore. "I couldn't pay you much, you know. Something derisory, in fact. Eight hundred."

He gave it no intonation of a question or proposition; he simply stopped talking after saying it.

Marcus took a moment to reply into the silence. "A thousand."

"We'll think about it," said Polydore, and this time, when Marcus expected a silence, went straight on: "Tell you what, if there was ever anything you wanted in my stock for yourself, you could have it at cost."

"I couldn't do that," said Marcus, ironically. "I'd feel I was taking bread out of your mouth."

"Well, let's say cost plus ten per cent," said Polydore without a second's pause, "up to the value of five hundred in any one calendar year, and cost plus twenty thereafter."

"All right," Marcus said, "on those terms I think my wife wants that Chinese carpet."

"I don't," said Nancy, like a schoolgirl.

Polydore, already making for the stairs, pretended not to have heard.

At the foot of the stairs he paused, sighed and said, "You can call me anything you like. If you come, I mean. Polydore. Mr Polydore. I'm usually called Uncle Polydore. So ageing. I sometimes think I've kept my figure for nothing. Or you can call me by my first name. I can't get used to saying christian name, though I *do* try. But I ought to warn you that it's Siegfried." He gave the first letter its proper German sound. "I'm not really a Wagnerian. Though often, as I mount these steps"—he flew at them—"I have thoughts of Walhalla."

"Goodbye," said Miss Scott-Marmion when they reached the top. And then, specially to Marcus, "I do hope you're going to come to us."

I I

MARCUS quickly elected to call Polydore Polly, a choice
which displeased Nancy, though she did not say so. Miss
Scott-Marmion he could not call anything until he got it
clear, which took him several months, that her name was
really Davina Heath-Plumpton. He recognised that his
original inability to grasp her name was a symptom that
he found her attractive and was resisting temptation; but
by then temptation had passed. She played no part in his
life, though she was always there, upstairs, usually on the
telephone to other young women, arranging to meet them
for luncheon in Wigmore Street.

Nancy took the whole thing—Marcus was not sure how.
He had the impression that she was not so much conceal-
ing her real opinion as trying to force her real opinion to
conform to his desire to accept the job; as though her most
real, deepest opinion of all was that it would be nasty of her
to raise objections. It was, it almost seemed, her own
character she was trying to alter. Immediately after their
interview with Polydore, she had said to Marcus, as soon
as they were enclosed in their own car,

"Well, darling, if you want to."

"There's no harm in giving it a try."

"No, quite," said Nancy. "You're not obliged to do it
for ever. In fact, that's one of the advantages of his offering so little. He can't expect you to stick it after you find
something that's more what you want."

After they reached home she said, in a manner which
confessed she had been thinking over not only the inter-

view but the comment she was now going to make,

"Most of the stuff he's got there is tripe."

"Not that Chinese carpet."

"No, but most of it."

"O, I don't know about *tripe*," said Marcus. "After all, just because we've got an austere flat—I mean, one's taste shouldn't get too austere. I think most of his stuff is not so much tripe as *tat*. After all, it's quite amusing."

"I don't think the joke will last you long," she said.

When he began actually to go out to work, Nancy shewed her goodwill—or, as Marcus interpreted it, her determination to feel goodwill—by building up for him, and cherishing him in, a setting of material comfort which might have been a satire on the Jewish respect for the male and the breadwinner, but which she did not, of course, intend satirically at all. Previously they had lived not only off scrubbed wood but out of tins: but now Marcus found that the kitchen, at least, was suddenly and very pleasantly furnished, and that Nancy had dug out the notebooks in which she had written down recipes and menus during her domestic science course.

The cooking Nancy had been taught was English and, in principle, not very interesting. Yet Nancy contrived to serve it with a neatness that was in itself a substitute for invention and part of the compliment to Marcus. There was a neatness in the pat of butter and sprinkling of parsley she slid with a palette knife on to the top of his fillet steak; there was a neatness about the shortcrust on her meat pies—and she was the only woman Marcus had known who was able to mix the exact amount of pastry she needed and did not have to use up the scraps in making coarse and untempting little pastry men with raisin eyes. Even so, she knew without his telling her that his tastes had begun to aspire beyond neatness; he would like to try out the exotic and the amusing. So she took a string shopping bag into Soho and began bringing him back prickly fruits which looked like animals and animals from alien seas that looked like succulent plants, together with multilingual instructions from the shopkeepers about how they should be prepared. Some of the instructions proved impractical and some of the foods dead sea fruits; but for others Marcus developed a gluttonous obsession.

Nancy had read that Italian housewives never bought factory-made *pasta* but made their own as English housewives made pastry. She went to an Italian restaurant and obliged the proprietor to take her into the kitchen and introduce her to his chef, from whom she obtained the recipe. She began to serve Marcus what he called a spaghetti *alla napolitana al paradiso*. She also wrote off to the daughter of the family she had stayed with in France, with whom she was still in desultory touch, and found out how the hams were cured in the family's country house. The curing took three days, and filled Nancy's and Marcus's flat with a smell evocative of provincial France, of whitewashed, sundrenched, shuttered, stone farmhouses—or of French films in which Marcus had seen such things—and which made Marcus wonder how he could live through the three days before the ham would be eatable. Sometimes in the middle of an afternoon in Polydore's basement he would lust for home.

The hams, once cured, were hung from hooks Nancy had had inserted in the ceiling in the kitchen, which was a big, sunny room and the one where Marcus and Nancy ate. It had been ruined by modernisation, its austere proportions demolished; and so it was the only room in the flat which did not present the problem of beauty.

When the winter began, Marcus's appetite increased and he put on a little weight.

Marcus indulged himself in the contrast between home and work like a sensualist inventing variations on the turkish bath. Work, because he did not need the money he earned, was a sort of play-acting, a daydream only slightly brisker than the usual kind. The very business of considering Polydore's furniture and objects from the amused point of view of what he could make of them—or, rather, of what he could, by a hey presto, make somebody else make of them—was like elaborating the details of a fantasy. It was as part of a pretence, or at least of something which did not cost him very much of his real life-energy, that he liked the feeling of his now firmer, more solid figure setting off to the shop, and liked the weariness and the ache for home in the limbs he dragged back through the dark to the light and comfort Nancy kept prepared.

Although the flat was not yet furnished, Nancy took care—it was part of the background to Marcus's work which she was compiling round them—to keep it warm. That was in contrast to the work itself. The stone basement under the shop was unheated. Polydore made neither apology nor attempt at a remedy; but in one of the tiny rooms upstairs he had a gas ring, and from time to time he would boil a kettle and—screeching of the perils of the stairs to a man carrying a tray—bring down mugs of Oxo to Marcus and the two men in overalls. Marcus did not think he brought them often enough. He would crouch in front of the piece he was working on and whistle, to himself but loud enough to mount the steps, "Polly put the kettle on."

But Polydore seemed to have had a childhood without nursery rhymes.

"Well, why don't you leave?" asked Nancy.

But Marcus preferred to drop Polydore a bigger hint. He asked his sister to knit him a jumper and when it was finished he turned up at work in ski pants, thick-knit jumper and a woolly cap which he kept on all day.

In the end Marcus told Polydore he would no longer come to work; the work must come to him.

Polydore refused. Next day Marcus stayed at home.

The day after, Polydore's station wagon stopped outside and the two men in overalls carried a drum-shaped card table, a tea chest and a firescreen up the stairs and into Marcus's and Nancy's flat.

Nancy watched him work all morning: that is to say, she watched him sit in front of the objects, sometimes getting up and running his hands over them. In the end he drew some diagrams, which he addressed to the firm in Fulham and which Nancy took out to the post.

In the afternoon it began to snow. Nancy and Marcus made love, magically, while the snowflakes pussy-footed down past their window.

"Darling, this is awful," she said, meaning the opposite. "If you're going to work at home, I'll have to get a job to go out to."

"I wish it snowed every day."

But, instead, it got warmer, and Marcus went back to work. However, he no longer worked regular hours. He would work, perhaps, three days a week at the shop and the rest at home, where furniture continued to be delivered and collected. He chose his home days in such a way that he was not bothered by the charwoman.

Going out to work, now that it was no longer new, ceased to please him specifically. But the furniture itself was still presenting him with fresh puzzles, which it pleased him to solve, and with fresh pleasures of sight and touch. The craftsmen and cabinet-makers of the past, like a confectioner of inexhaustible invention, poured their sweets into his experience; he preferred home as the place where he might taste them without hurry or formality; and sometimes as he explored a new piece he really did make sucking sounds with his mouth, as though it was only by softening, dissolving and assimilating an idea of the object that he could possess the delight it afforded him.

The furniture—or, rather, the turnover of furniture—

was presumably why the flat did not get furnished in its own right. The Chinese carpet it did acquire. Marcus had intended to forgo it, as a gesture to Nancy. It was she who, lamenting one day their unfurnished state, asked him if it was still in Polydore's stock. Marcus had it delivered in the van along with the itinerant furniture. Polydore did not charge him the ten per cent above cost because Marcus at the same time compensated Polydore's stock, by selling him his Chinese bowl for what he had given for it. Nancy had agreed there was no place for it in the flat. Marcus sold his seicento painting in the saleroom, making a profit of two hundred per cent. His statuette was shoved away in a cupboard.

Thanks to Polydore's furniture, the flat lost its empty look. Polydore would often send fresh consignments without asking for the previous ones back; some largish pieces stayed with Nancy and Marcus for months at a stretch.

"You realise," Nancy said, "he's using this place as an extra store?"

"Well, does that matter?" said Marcus. "We have the use of the stuff."

Having the use of it gave their flat something of the interestingly full quality of Polydore's real store; and perhaps it was that which made it so comfortable.

"But none of it's *ours*," Nancy objected. They could, of course, have bought any or all of the pieces. But none of them was just right: and that again perhaps contributed to the feeling of comfort. "It's like living in lodgings," she said.

"But what classy ones!" Marcus replied. "Our landlady must be—what? At least a white Russian Countess, don't you think?"

But Nancy did not like sharing the flat even with a white Russian figment and brushed her aside.

Marcus explained that it was useful to him to have

84

plenty of time to brood over the pieces before working on them. "I like to live with them. Really, I like to sit with them." He even told her that, with wood furniture in particular, since wood *was* organic, *was*, indeed, part of a tree, the only way to get the feel of it properly was to sit and watch it grow, like a tree.

Nancy obviously thought the idea factitious if not affected, and she treated it with impatience.

But Marcus really was settling into a domestic version of a rustic slowness. Once he had mentioned sitting with the furniture, Nancy noticed that he sat a great deal. What had been, when she first knew him, the hint of a stammer or splutter in his speech had withdrawn but had left its space behind it, so that there was now a brief silence before each of his phrases. These pauses, which could no longer be construed as hesitancy or self-distrust, but only as a slightly ironic, teasing laziness, had the effect of thickening his speech. His sentences advanced on you deliberately, like a furry caterpillar; and often they intended to tickle. There was even the suspicion of a lisp in his speech. Although the two manners were so utterly different, the one flattering and always on the point of flight, the other thick and padded, Nancy was certain that the lisp had been caught from Polydore.

Another contagion was the habit of comfortable cardigans in colours which, Marcus was persuaded, would not shew any spots that fell on them. But they did shew: a glitter of dried glue; a few freckles of gold leaf rubbed into the ribbing. Nancy was always scrubbing at his clothes, sometimes in the sink, sometimes with her thumbnail while he was wearing them. "Lady Macbeth," he said.

His fingers—splayed, perhaps, by fitting intricate little bits of wood into place and pressing them firm until the glue set—developed plump little cushions at the tips; they looked like the fingers of one of the frogs which have suckers for clinging to tree trunks or to the back of the female. They had not lost their sensitive appearance; but it was no longer the sensitivity of avoiding contact with substances; now, they seemed to move deliberately, though still lightly, to any substance which presented itself and to take in its texture through the pores—to appreciate, almost to listen to, textures and consistencies.

Because their dining room, although full of furniture, was not furnished, Nancy and Marcus could not ask people to dinner—at least "not", as Nancy put it, "*people*: because I'm damned if I'm going to tell my guests they mustn't spill the wine on the table because the table isn't ours." They could entertain only such people as could be invited to eat in the kitchen. That would have included Marcus's mother, of course, were it not that she had a distrust of food not cooked by herself. She preferred Nancy and Marcus to come to her; when she did visit them in Chelsea, it was for tea, where she ate nothing. Nancy's parents they did not invite because of the embarrassment about whether to invite them together or separately. They both seemed too weary to sustain a whole dinner and conversation with one another. It was easier for the four of them to go every now and then to a recital at the Wigmore Hall—where Marcus could so simply buy the tickets during his lunch hour. Then he, Nancy and Nancy's father would wait in the at first crowded and then emptied foyer for Nancy's mother, who always arrived at the last moment, rushed, hurrying herself in from a rainy night outside, and the four of them would slide into the auditorium one second before the music began; whereupon the separating effect of music would take charge and isolate each of them into a little listening centre, as though each one carried his own receiving set and wore his own earphones, so that they did not have to behave as a group, let alone a family, all evening. Orchestral music, Marcus thought, might have bludgeoned them, by its very beat and brassiness, into a communal response; but since it was always chamber music, the thin, exact tones, each quite finite and without reverberation, moved drily towards them and enclosed each person in his own linear, unbreakable confine. Marcus remembered how the parents had stolen into the drawing room of their own house to listen to music, like the animals in *The Magic Flute*. Now it seemed to him that they all four stole separately into the Wigmore Hall and, when the music was over, stole separately out again.

That left Marcus's sister who could be invited to sit in the warm kitchen, under the hams, over prolonged meals: and Polydore. He had arrived one evening after Marcus had spent the day at home, to ask after one of the pieces Marcus was working on; and he had stayed until the smell of cooking was so indecent that they had to invite him to dinner. After that, he began dropping in once a week, and since it was obvious he was going to come in any case they thought they might as well invite him in so many words, which at least prevented him from coming when it was inconvenient. He was gluttonous. He would endure even the deliberate discomfort of Nancy's welcome to get at her cooking. He ate and ate and ate and remained as thin as ever.

They were awkward evenings. Marcus addressed him as Polly and made jokes with him or talked shop. Nancy said little and addressed him as Siegfried, with the proper German z sound.

Nancy did not, in fact, like either of her guests. With Marcus's sister, even Marcus did not attempt to talk much. She always brought her knitting, and after coffee she would push her chair back, take out her knitting, shake it clear of the empty cups and sit knitting over the table. In bed after one of her visits Nancy said to Marcus:

"I've discovered what it is I dislike about her."

"What?"

"She's got breasts."

"Well," said Marcus in his new, slow manner, "it would be a little monstrous if she hadn't."

"Yes but, don't you see," Nancy said, "she looks so like you, darling, in some ways. And then I look at her and suddenly see she's got woman's breasts, instead of nice flat strong ones, like yours"—which she kissed.

Polydore she disliked most when he made Marcus talk shop. He bought a length of green silk, figured with a chinoiserie motif, which one of the other shops in Wigmore Street had had copied from an eighteenth-century material to the order of a customer. The customer had backed out but was too influential to sue. Besides, a law suit would have cost more than the loss on the silk, as Polydore knew; so when he heard of it he offered a very small price indeed and held out, and in the end the other shop was glad to let him have the stuff. He brought the bale with him to dinner and asked Marcus's advice about which of their pieces they should cover with it. When Nancy came back into the drawing room to tell them dinner was ready, she found that Marcus, though offering no advice, was on his knees in front of the chair over which he had opened out the silk and was, as Nancy later told him she thought of it, with his body worshipping the silk. His head was immersed. When he heard her come in he—without looking up—held out a fold to her between his fingers, like an oriental offering a morsel from his own plate. "Come and *feel* it, darling."

"Get up," she said, in the traditional manner of a Victorian lady receiving a proposal of marriage from a physically repugnant suitor; but adding: "You look like an old Jew merchant."

"I *am* an old Jew merchant," Marcus slowly said.

"Aren't we all, dear," Polydore fluttered at her, "if you scratch us, I mean."

Again Nancy kept her comment for bed. "I hate him when he pretends not to be Jewish."

88

"But don't *we*?"

"No, of course not. I mean, obviously we can't practise the Jewish *religion*, because we don't believe in religion."

"I don't see there's much else to it," Marcus said. "The whole business was religious in the first place. If we've dropped *that* . . ."

"There's plenty else to it."

"Well, I suppose I could get a plastic surgeon to alter my nose."

She caressed him. "I wouldn't have a surgeon touch you."

"A surgeon did touch me. When I was a baby."

"He wouldn't, if I'd been there to stop him," said Nancy. "I resent any diminution of you. Particularly, darling, *there*."

He wondered again, and quite explicitly this time, how she could have such a satirically affectionate sense of amusement in bed and none whatever out of bed. But since he was *in* bed when he wondered, he did not pursue the answer.

They did not go abroad that summer, although it was hot. They slept under a sheet and often woke spontaneously in the small hours because the temperature had dropped; but instead of pulling up a blanket to cover them they applied to one another. Marcus could plunge himself into Nancy with all the delicious casualness of a man lying on a river bank and lazily inserting his bare leg in the warm stream, sensitive to, delighted by, the pulsing of the vigorous current against it.

12

In the autumn Nancy took a part-time job, offered her by someone she knew, and Marcus took up smoking.

"But why *now*?" Nancy asked. "You've gone so many years without."

"I don't know," he said. "I suppose it's calming."

"You don't need calming. You're almost worryingly calm these days."

"Well, it's easy somehow. I suppose because Polly does it."

He smoked the same short thin ones—too loosely packed to be called slender—as Polydore, and got them into the same browned stumps.

Nancy's job was with a small music publisher whose premises were somewhere off Great Marlborough Street. Marcus usually lost his way when he went to call for her. And when he did come on it, it was a disconcerting place: half office—Nancy worked upstairs—and half shop. The shop window was a large uncoloured space containing some sheet music for the piano, a couple of miniature scores, an ocarina and the smallest available size of the bust of Beethoven. The interior was even more disconcerting: a dim, empty silence, in which Marcus stood uneasily until he was offered help ("I've only come to collect my wife") by one of several slight nervous youths who worked there and who seemed to talk in soft voices to shew their appreciation of serious music.

"It's not much of a job," Nancy admitted. "They said it would be useful that I can read music, but it's never been yet. Still, I do at least meet a few people."

At first one of the people she sometimes met was Marcus—they lunched together; but they were just beyond easy walking distance from each other; and after a while Nancy began making appointments with other people, and Marcus found it more convenient to go to a nearby pub with Polydore. He never felt he had seen *her* after lunching with her and one of her friends.

Nancy was conveniently placed to shop in Soho; and she had taken only a part-time job expressly so that Marcus's comfort should not suffer.

13

"Darling, you really must get thinner."

"All my life," Marcus said, tapping the metal end of his pencil on his teeth and continuing to sit in front of an early Victorian occasional table, "people have been telling me I must get fatter."

From the way he threw the emphasis on to the front of the sentence and left the end to be taken for granted, Nancy could tell he really had misheard.

"But I didn't say fatter."

"O." He broke his dream and looked down with amusement at his waistband. "O, no, of course not. Yes, I'd noticed. I can hardly get into some of my clothes."

At first it had been merely a more pronounced look, not even unappealing, to the buttocks. Then a plumpness, still quite becoming, had appeared below his waist. A heaviness had gathered on his hips, all the way round. And now, when he sat closely crouched, as he liked to do when he worked on the furniture, you could see that the upper part of his trouser legs was wholly occupied, was bulging and undulating, with his thighs.

It was all the more noticeable because he so seldom wore a suit but went about in odd trousers and one of his soiled cardigans.

"You must cut down on carbohydrates."

"All right. But you feed me too well."

"Then I'll cut down on them for you. But you must co-operate at lunch time."

"Look what a lot Polly eats," Marcus said. "I shall

never believe again that justice is a natural principle."

"Did you ever?"

"Probably not. I haven't many principles. I cut down on them some time ago." He lit a cigarette.

"Your fingers are getting stained," Nancy said.

"Yes, I know. I'll try some of my lemon juice on them." He sometimes used lemon juice to bring up painted furniture.

At first Nancy went on making the same sort of meals as usual, and simply gave Marcus a plate from which carbohydrates had been omitted. But he would open his dog's eyes at her and plead; and if she did manage to resist him he would prospect round the kitchen after dinner and, without the smallest subterfuge, pick up something and eat it in his fingers.

She had great difficulty persuading him bread was carbohydrate.

"I'm sure it isn't," he said. "How do you know?"

"Well, *darling*. When I did that domestic science course we had to go into dietetics quite seriously."

He cut himself an elbow end from a long loaf. "I'm sure the crust can't be fattening."

"I see we shall both have to diet," Nancy said. "So long as the stuff's in the house, you'll be at it."

"We can't have a house without bread. I feel rather peasant about it. A house without bread isn't home."

"Then you'll just have to camp out. Even more," she added, "than we do at present. We *must* get the place furnished some time."

He could not understand why, since she was in this mood, she did not go on to say he must get a decent job, too.

Nancy began to diet both herself and him at home. But the rules had to be relaxed when Marcus's sister or Polydore came to dinner; and Marcus took pleasure in helping himself to more bread and more butter in the course of the meal, knowing that Nancy would not rebuke him while a guest was there. Moreover, even she, who could calculate a quantity of pastry so precisely, could not buy a loaf exactly the size for four unpredictable appetites at one meal. There was always bread left over next morning; and although Marcus did not like to sit down to it at breakfast face to face and alone with Nancy, he seemed to think that what he ate standing up did not count. While she washed up, he would wander round the kitchen nibbling bits of bread. If Nancy looked round at him, she would receive an ironical look; if she turned to face him squarely he would give her what he deliberately made an appealing, urchin grin.

"I won't be reduced to snatching it out of your hand," she said, "like a slum mother."

But she *was* reduced to rolls: when a guest was coming she bought, instead of a loaf, precisely three rolls. If either of their habitual guests had felt meanly treated and had come no more, she would not have minded.

Marcus made up for his own deprivations during his lunch hours in the pub with Polydore. The pub offered a choice between carbohydrates: cold pasty, with a sprinkling of mince and gristle inside; or sandwiches containing a flavour of meat paste. The only other food available was pickled onions. Nancy had told Marcus they were fattening. Marcus suggested to Polydore that they find another pub. But Polydore liked the familiar one, and it was near.

Before Nancy had begun to diet him, Marcus had disliked the sort of food the pub provided and had often eaten nothing at lunch time. Nowadays, however, he was so hungry that he ate it in quantities. He would order three or four large pickled onions to be lifted out of the lumpish glass jar. The pub did not possess a barmaid, which was another reason why Polydore liked it; but when Marcus watched the delicately pink plastic tongs descend into the jar, behind whose thick glass they looked almost pickled themselves, he felt that in colour, coldness and genteelly fishing fastidiousness they were an apt substitute for a barmaid's fingers. Moved by imagining this old-fashioned barmaid he one day ordered a glass of stout, which he decided would be her favourite drink, though she would consider port more ladylike. After that he began to drink stout regularly. He found it allayed his appetite better than other drinks: and his sense of irony could not help taking its name as a tiny, harmless weapon against Nancy.

Polydore, content that Marcus's new taste was inexpensive, became punctilious about paying for rounds and was always urging Marcus to drink another stout.

"I mustn't. Nancy doesn't like it."

"Does she find it working-class of you?" Polydore asked, giggling.

"I suppose she must." He did not like to tell Polydore the true reason because Polydore himself was so unsightly thin.

These days Marcus told Nancy he smoked because it helped to curb his appetite. But smoking did not curb it at all; and in any case he was satisfying it at lunch time.

In January there was a hard frost, and Marcus, although he had refused to go to work in Polydore's basement, wanted to wear his ski pants and jumper for working at home. But he could no longer get into them. He kept warm by wearing his bedroom slippers and his dressing gown over his ordinary clothes. But when his sister came she found the flat too hot in any case and could not think why Marcus needed extra clothing. "I should have thought your embonpoint would keep you warm."

"He's cold because he never takes any exercise," Nancy said.

Nancy chose that evening, and seemed to have chosen the presence—as witness? he wondered—of his sister, in which to tell him that some people called the Rosenfelds, whom she sometimes lunched with, were having a man to stay—a publisher of art books, who was flying over, for a couple of days, from Switzerland, where he had his head-quarters; but his business was really a pan-European combine, which specialised in first-class colour work, to which texts were fitted in half a dozen languages.

Marcus, not only interpreting her drift at once but feeling a need to defend himself, replied:

"I don't want to be an art publisher, and flying about Europe in a plane doesn't count as exercise."

Nancy said nothing more about it for a week, when:

"The Rosenfelds have asked us to dinner," she told him.

"O."

"While *he's* there."

"O."

"Marcus, I was *awful*."

"How do you mean?" he asked—affectionately, because she was distressed.

"I was pushing. I virtually squeezed the invitation out of them."

"Then we'd better tart up," he said friendly, "so as not to disappoint them. I hope my good suit still fits."

It just did, all except the waistcoat, which Nancy let out at the back.

The frost relaxed, and Marcus went back to work at the shop. Nancy made him promise to be home early, "in *plenty* of time", on the night of the dinner party.

He was punctual, and in case this surprised her he explained:

"I'm looking forward to it. I shall be allowed a decent meal for once." In fact, he had already eaten plenty, while he was out.

Nancy was already dressed and was making up.

"We've got ages yet," he said. "If you put on your eye-shadow now it'll fade before we get there."

"Not if I powder over it. I want to give it time to settle."

"Won't the powder hide it?"

"Not the quantities I'm putting on."

"Careful," he said, looking at her reflexion over her shoulder. "You don't want to *look* pushing."

"I may as well," she said. "*You* never will."

"Don't you think he'll offer me a partnership on the spot?"

She did not answer, but it might have been because she had just started on her mouth.

He wandered round the bedroom for a bit, smelling the cosmetics she had got out for the occasion.

"If you've nothing else to do, you might try that lemon juice on your hands."

"I tried it," he said. "Weeks ago. It didn't work."

She did her hair.

"You ought to start to get ready, Marcus."

"I'm afraid I feel awful."

"There's nothing to be scared of. No one could think *you* were angling for a job."

"I mean I feel ill."

"Where?"

"Head. And rather faint."

"Lie down for ten minutes. We're in plenty of time."

He lay on the bed, his hands behind his head, and watched her giving an extra smoothing to the foundation on her neck.

"How do you feel?"

"Bloody, I'm afraid."

She came and stood beside him, looking at him hard, and then walked into the bathroom and came back with the thermometer.

"This used to be——" he began, with the thermometer under his tongue; but she told him not to talk.

She took the thermometer out and read it.

"What does it say?"

"A hundred and two."

He just lay, looking up at her. She just stood.

"I must wash the thermometer," she said eventually. "You get undressed and get into bed."

"O no, I'm coming," he answered, beginning to struggle up, and putting more energy than he need into the struggle for fear of being thought feigning.

"Don't be silly."

"I can take a couple of aspirins."

"Don't be silly. It might *be* something. I must wash the thermometer and ring the Rosenfelds. Is it all right if I go? They may think it odd if I don't, after I made such a fuss to get asked."

"Yes of course it's all right. If you don't mind going alone."

She took his temperature twice more before she left, as though she could not believe the thermometer. At the last reading, his temperature had risen by half a degree.

She offered to bring him some food to eat while she was out; but for once he genuinely did not want food.

When she saw him actually snuggled down under a hump of blankets she shewed a spasm of tenderness and, so well as she could while preserving her make-up, kissed him.

He gave her, over the foldback of the sheet, the urchin grin he had perfected.

"I was telling you, this used to be one of my daydreams when I was at school. It was a daydream for gym days. 'Nonsense' says matron, and slips the thermometer briskly under my tongue. She takes it out and reads it, while I look up at her with listless eyes from my pillow. 'My God,' she cries, 'call the doctor and the headmaster. A hundred and twelve point five.'"

"A thermometer only goes to a hundred and ten," Nancy said as she left the flat.

She came home early, disappointed, and worried about Marcus, whose temperature she took at once. It was still a hundred and two point five.

"Didn't he take one look and say, 'I can tell from a glance at you that your enterprising young husband is just the man for me'?"

"You're too good at daydreams. It's the fever. No, he didn't."

She made herself a bed of cushions on the floor so as not to disturb his night.

In the morning his temperature was normal.

But he stayed in bed for another two days, in case it had been something. Nancy temporarily relaxed his diet and brought him trays of the sort of food he liked. His view of her from the bed, as she carried away the emptied trays, was all of neat hips and bottom in a neat suit, neat dark brown seam down the back of her legs, neat dark blue back to the not foolishly high-heeled court shoes. It put him in mind of an air hostess. On the last day of his convalescence he said to her, slyly:

"Of course, one never knows how far these things are psycho-somatic."

"No. One doesn't."

"I expect I just wanted to give myself the illusion of being a disgustingly fat old high-pressure publisher, flying round Europe with a cigar in my mouth, and making a pass at the air hostess." He put out the cigarette which was what had really been in his mouth and, when Nancy next approached him—to straighten the sheets—did make a pass at her, and drew her down into the bed with him.

When he was up and about again, back on his diet and back at work (he began going to the shop more regularly, because it made it easier for him to satisfy his appetite in the lunch hour), he said to Nancy:

"Don't be too disgruntled about old whatsit." He

meant the publisher. "Surely he'll have to come to England again quite soon?"

"I can't force another invitation out of the Rosenfelds."

"There are other approaches."

"You don't seem to realise we can't ask people to dinner here, while we're not furnished."

Her tone seemed to signal that she had given up trying to make him an art publisher. Accepting this, he made arrangements, a day or two later, to put some of his capital into Polydore's business.

"But *why?*" Nancy asked.

"It's a good business."

"No better than hundreds of others."

"We're lucky to have the chance," Marcus said. "He's not a public company. Where the money was, it was making four and a half per cent. With Polly it'll make ten or twelve."

"Well at least will you insist on having some control over what he does?"

"I've got all the control I need. He hardly buys at all without asking my advice."

"Aren't you going to make him expand? He could get a second shop."

"Who'd run it?"

"You."

Marcus shook his head.

"Darling, he can't expect you to go on being a manual worker. You can't stay in his basement for ever."

"That's what I'm good at. He's good at the other things. It's piece of luck for me."

"But you could buy him up."

Marcus chuckled. "I daresay I will one day. But there's no hurry."

14

NANCY came back several times to the question of furnishing the flat, not because of inviting people to dinner but for its own sake.

"Do you hate me to go on about it, Marcus?"

"No. But these things take time."

"Do you think I'm getting obsessed?"

"No. But I don't think it's so important. We're marvellously comfortable as things are. There seems to be a sort of fashion for young married couples to make a fetish of their flats. Especially childless couples. It's a bit pathetic."

Nancy asked:

"Do you think we ought to have a child?"

He took even longer than usual to answer, surprised by the question.

"There's no ought. It's a thing we can do what we like about. And since it's you who'll have to have it, it's for you to say."

"Sometimes I feel a certain pressure from the prospective grandparents. Especially your mother."

"O damn that. She hasn't dared say anything, has she?"

"No, of course not. Just wistful looks."

"She can give those to her other child. Why can't *she* get married again, and supply hundreds of grandchildren? She could certainly knit for hundreds."

"I've always felt odd about having a child," Nancy said. "I never thought I would have one."

A day or two later, Nancy said:

"Should we give it a try?"

"What?"

"A baby. I mean, we could stop trying *not* to have one. And see what happens."

"Yes. All right," he said in his mild, amenable slow voice.

"It may not happen."

"No. It may not happen."

But the child was conceived the first time they gave it the opportunity.

"We belong to a philoprogenitive race," Marcus said.

They telephoned the news to the three grandparents. Next time Marcus's sister came to dinner in Chelsea, she brought a present. Marcus was surprised to feel through the wrapping paper that it was a book. It was a great chunky American volume the size of a desk encyclopaedia, illustrated on every page—"lavishly", the dust jacket said —with shiny colour photography that reminded him of the seicento painting he had sold; its title was *Traditional Jewish Food*.

Marcus did not know whether his sister meant it as a protest against the non-sectarian menus she shared once a week in their house or as an indication of how the baby should be brought up.

Dinner, not by Nancy's and Marcus's wish, was turned into an acknowledgement of the baby. Marcus's sister not only made more effort to talk than usual but talked, with complimentary speculations, about the baby. She called down enough sense of social occasion to prompt them all, instead of sitting on in the kitchen after the meal, to return to the drawing room.

Sunk in a sofa which was Polydore's latest loan, Marcus picked up from its arm the cookery book—or, as it preferred to be called, cook book—and began looking at the pictures. "No, really," he said, slowly, teasing his sister, "this is disgraceful. Americans would talk about anything.

I mean, if being Jewish is no longer something to be ashamed of——"

Nancy cut straight across him. "You're being quite absurd, Marcus. And grossly unfair."

Both he and his sister were amazed. After a silence, he felt obliged to say something more to his sister about her present. But his mind could not jump out of the chaffing groove it had started in. "It's certainly mouthwatering," he said. "What a present for a man who's on a diet."

Two weeks later, however, he was no longer on a diet. Nancy had to put the idea aside, because pregnancy gave her an insatiable appetite herself.

15

WHEN she was two months pregnant, Nancy confessed to him that she had always felt a physical terror of giving birth to a child. "Partly it's physical cowardice," she said, "but there's something else as well. It's more than just a rational fear."

"Well I don't think it's very surprising. I should think most women feel the same."

"I don't know." She appeared to disclaim knowledge of other women. "Or perhaps I do know. Some women are afraid of losing their virginity, some women are afraid of having a baby. I took the first in my stride——"

"You couldn't," he consideringly interposed, "have chosen a better place to take it."

Nancy burst into tears.

When he apologetically and gently dabbed her tears with his handkerchief, she told him that her reaction meant nothing; it was a symptom of nothing except pregnancy, which made her edgy and weepy. All the medical booklets she had bought on the subject said that the lodging of the fœtus in the wall of the womb produced a physical shock to the whole organism.

16

AT three months, shock, weepiness, delicacy were all swallowed up in euphoria. Even the physical fear was dwarfed.

"No doubt *the* day will be absolutely bloody," Nancy said, "but it can't last for ever, and afterwards we'll have *it*."

"I find it impossible to imagine what *it* will be like."

"Of course you do. You're not even allowed to know what sex it will be. Because, if people could imagine it all in advance, no one would do it."

"Do you think," Marcus asked, "that the lodging of *it* within the walls of this house will produce a shock to *my* organism?"

"Undoubtedly," she replied. "It might even make you thin. Running round to get its nappies up on the line."

At the beginning of pregnancy, her appetite had been bitter, miserable, an addiction. Now it became glorious. She spent half the day cooking and at night they sat down to banquets. Whereas he was even further slowing down, she became even more, became Wagnerianly, energetic. She would not hear of giving up her job till the last moment. "I've never felt so well." During the meals she was always jumping up, to fetch another loaf, to look at the next course in the oven.

The curious thing was that she didn't get fat. It was Marcus who swelled as the pregnancy progressed. In Nancy it did not shew.

"I don't believe you *are* pregnant."

"The best medical opinion in London says I am." She said it like a boast.

She put on one of the maternity smocks she had bought, along with the medical booklets, at the outset, but Marcus made her take it off, saying she looked obscene, like a little girl masquerading. "It's more for me than you," he added.

The only things she would not cook or eat were the Jewish dishes catalogued in Marcus's sister's present to them. Marcus went through the pages with a curiosity partly scientific (under the name of each dish, the Yiddish name was given in italics, like the scientific under the common name of an animal) and partly gluttonous. "Don't you think you ought to try some of them? At least when she comes?"

"Perhaps—afterwards," Nancy said. "I don't want to take any risks with my digestion at the moment."

"Your digestion seems to stand up to quite a lot of punishment."

"I know," she said, happily. "You'd think I'd get fat from eating, if not from the baby."

"You're like Polly," he said. Nancy was not so displeased as she would have been before. "Do you think Polly's pregnant?"

"Not unless you made him so," Nancy said.

She gave other signs, too, that although her euphoria had not lessened her dislike of Polydore, it had given her a freedom—and therefore a sort of gaiety—in expressing it.

If she had had, before, a talent for sexual intercourse, she now seemed to have an appetite for it. For the first time Marcus felt an impulse to flinch from her sexually. He did not think he was withdrawing from the strong physicalness of her well being, or even from the just perceptible coarsening of her face, which was the only way the pregnancy had yet made itself bodily visible. But the idea had fixed itself in his mind that when he made love to Nancy the baby was spying on them.

In any other circumstances he would have explained his feeling to Nancy. But then in any other circumstances he would not have felt it.

She, so far from noticing an inhibition on his part, delighted in explaining to him that by making her pregnant he had destroyed in her the last shred of sexual inhibition. "At any other time one must have, at the back of one's mind, the fear of getting pregnant. One always knows something *might* go wrong. The only one hundred per cent foolproof contraceptive is to have a baby already in there."

Her words did nothing to demolish his image of being spied on.

Only in the seventh month did she begin to need her smocks. "You're an honest pregnant woman at last." But it was still a small pregnancy and gave her not the least trouble to carry round, sticking out in front of her in a shape like a rugger ball. "You won't be disappointed if you give birth to a small rugger ball?"

"I won't be disappointed," she said, "whatever I give birth to."

She made the same reply when Marcus's sister asked whether to buy pink or blue knitting wool.

But when the term grew nearer, she told Marcus that she really wanted a girl.

"I didn't think you much liked girls."

"I told you once before," she said, laughing, "ages ago, it's different when it's me. And it'll be different when it's mine."

He thought she was probably rebelling against the obsessive Jewish desire for sons; and, in case she should misinterpret him, he did not admit to her that he would prefer a boy.

Presently he thought that perhaps she did not so much

want a girl as want to avoid a boy, on whom the Jewish pressure would be much stronger. Nancy did not say anything about it, so in the end he asked:

"If it should be a boy, would we have him circumcised?"

"I don't know. What do you think? I suppose it's quite a sensible hygienic precaution, anyway. Lots of non-Jews do."

"You told me once before, ages ago, that things of that sort aren't hygienic precautions at all."

She said nothing. Even her euphoria could not quite ride over his quoting her own words at her to an end that was not meant to be amusing. He was aware of hostility in his own speech; and it led him to a prevision that, if they did have a son, they might, over him, become hostile to one another.

17

BUT it was a girl.

Nancy was delivered of her, almost punctually, which all the medical books told them was rare with a first child, with a great deal of effort but very little actual pain. She had taken tuition, of course, and done her exercises regularly. The only way she departed from the advice given at her classes was to ask Marcus not to be present at the birth.

The midwife told him immediately afterwards that his wife was very good at having babies. He replied he had known she would be. Nancy was very pleased when he reported the conversation: she set store on the midwife's approval.

Polydore bought a half bottle of champagne and ordered it to be mixed with Marcus's usual stout.

In the hospital Nancy still seemed borne up by her euphoria—or perhaps by the midwife's approval. But when she brought the baby home she fell subject to weariness. She remained weary even when she gave up breastfeeding the child. She worried about her weariness, about her unwillingness to drag herself round in the baby's service and—as soon as the baby took to the bottle—about the fact that it was rapidly proving overweight. In this last worry Marcus read a reproach to himself. For a day or two he ate less. But Nancy was too tired to work out diets for him—she was content if she could only serve *some* food—and in any case he reckoned that if he had really passed on an hereditary disposition to overweight it would not be cured by reducing the symptom in himself.

The baby seemed to him a very elementary form of life, hardly more organised than a sea invertebrate. Its life activity provoked no thoughts or imaginings in him: it merely went on impressing the absolute primacy of eating and excretion. All the same he was conscious of—in an elementary way—loving it. This consciousness came to him only when he thought about the question in the abstract, not at all in the moments when he held the baby in his arms and on his knee, where Nancy sometimes deposited it while she prepared its bottle; at those moments all he thought of was its eating and excreting.

He could not conceive why they had wasted time speculating about its sex or why he had supposed its sex might cause discord between him and Nancy. The thing that had come into the flat *had* no sex.

Nancy had preserved her figure, but she had not got her looks back. Her face still had the coarseness of pregnancy but without the healthiness. Her weariness shewed. It was perhaps not surprising that her plainness made Marcus feel constantly tender towards her; what did surprise him was it repeatedly provoked him to passion. It was as though her good looks had been a touch too neat and contained for a completely abandoned experience; he had always remained sensuously aware of the niceness of her body. Now he thought it would be possible to lose awareness of both bodies.

Nancy, however, did not share this experience. She did not see her return home in the same terms of sexual welcome as he did. She saw it as a list of things to be done. She worried in case she failed to do them. "I may be good at *producing* babies, but I'm not much good at following it up." *He* was worried in case her newly-found talent for giving birth should obscure the earlier one for sexual intercourse.

He had been afraid the embryo was spying on them: she

was afraid the baby was—not eavesdropping, but needing her. He knew she was aware she would feel guilty if, at the moment when she was seeking her own pleasure, the baby should wake up and bawl one of its monotonous two needs. She made love with one ear on it, as though it were an undependable alarm clock, in the next room. "Darling, am I very dreary for you at the moment?"

"No, of course not. I'm sorry if I force myself on you." It was like a moment's return to his old, hopeless, self disparagement.

"You don't. Don't be silly."

He felt almost a romantic ache towards her, as though she were unattainable. And in truth, although she made herself—almost dutifully, he felt—attainable bodily, he had to be content with satisfactions for his body only. They sent him to sleep, but like an anaesthetic. In the end, he became tired all the time, too.

Nancy had decided the child was to be called Claire. He did not much like the name, but he had nothing against it. In any case he could not really feel the force of giving the child a name at all, while it remained so elementary. It seemed whimsical to give it an attribute of personality, like nicknaming a mollusc.

He bought the child an old-fashioned wooden cradle which Polydore had spotted in the sale room. Although it was connected with Polydore, Nancy thought the cradle pretty; but she kept the child in its carrycot. "I hope you don't mind, darling. But the cradle seems too nice to spoil. And it would make so much extra work if I had to scrub it out every time she wet her nappy."

"No, I don't mind."

"There's enough to do as it is. I must get you back on to a diet, darling. But just at the moment it seems too much to work out three separate menus. *With* everything else."

"You ought to get an au pair girl," he said. "That's

what other people do. Though I must say, I don't know how they go about it."

Nancy of course did. "You go to an agency and ask for one who's already had a job over here and didn't like it. It makes them more grateful for being treated decently. You get one who's been exploited in Finchley and writes, 'Not North London' on the application form."

"But," Marcus slowly said, "that obviously means 'Not Jews'."

"Well," Nancy said, "if they're hypocritical enough to write 'Not North London' when they mean 'Not Jews', then in their own sense of the word we're not Jews."

"But I don't want an anti-Semite living with us," he said.

"We needn't have anyone," said Nancy.

Two days later, however, he told her she must. "It's stupid not to. We've got the extra room. It's stupid for you to do it all when you needn't."

"All right. I'll go to the agency. I can take the pram."

"But not a German girl," he said.

"We'll have to see what they've got."

"Not German."

"Which is worse," Nancy asked, " 'Not Jews' or 'Not Germans'?"

"I know damn well which I think is worse."

"I think you're unreasonable," she said. "The sort of girl we'd get was only five or six in 1945."

"That's what they all say."

"No doubt because it's true of them all."

"They've got parents, haven't they? They come here from families. They write home. We might even find ourselves exchanging civilities with the parents."

"Are you responsible for everything your parents have done?"

"My parents never did anything like that."

The agency sent three girls to be interviewed.

"The Judgment of Paris," said Marcus.

Nancy knew he had the Rubens picture in mind.

"We can't see them all together," she said, "and I'm afraid you mustn't ask them to undress."

"Then I shall leave it to you. I can't judge in such restricted circumstances."

Of the French girl, who came first, he said:

"No one would want to ask her to undress."

The second girl, who was Norwegian, was plump and friendly and looked forty-five.

Only the last girl was German. She was rather remarkably beautiful.

After they had all been, Nancy said:

"Well, Paris?"

"I leave it to you. I never thought I'd make a shepherd anyway."

"D'you still feel, 'Not German'?"

"I leave it to you."

Nancy engaged the beautiful girl, of course. It was part of making Marcus comfortable. Marcus never remembered to ask Nancy whether the girl was one of those who had written "Not North London" on the application form.

18

THE German girl was called Ilse—which was also the name of Marcus's sister. Or, rather, it was his sister's real name, which their mother still used: among her own friends she had long before anglicised it to Elsie. Only Nancy, on discovering the real form of the name by marrying into the family, chose to revert to it sometimes—not in order to annoy Marcus's sister, though it did annoy her, but in the hope of liking her better under a less displeasing name.

The German Ilse could not move in until a week after Nancy had engaged her. She had to work out the notice she had given at her present job. Marcus spent the week repenting. "I think I'm going to hate having someone living with us." "You didn't feel that about the baby." "No. But *she's* Jewish." Nancy spent it getting a room ready for the girl. "We can't put *her* in with Siegfried's furniture."

Because the workmen would have taken too long, they prepared the room themselves and bought a bed, a desk, a chair and a little wall bookcase from Peter Jones's. Like all au pair girls—so Nancy told Marcus—Ilse was learning English at a school for foreigners and preparing for the Cambridge examination. The whole key to her social position, her character, even how they should treat her, was, Nancy said, contained in the word *student*. Hence the desk and the bookshelf.

Marcus thought it a pity to paper the walls they had originally stripped: but of course it was not their own taste they were consulting but what they imagined to be student taste. Yet when they finished the room Nancy said:

"In a way, I think it's the prettiest room in the flat. At least all the stuff is our own."

"Well tell the girl not to come, and we'll move in here."

"It's too small for a double bed."

The room, being spare, had housed quite a lot of Polydore's furniture; and now that that had been moved out Nancy found the rest of the place cluttered.

"I don't feel it as cluttered," Marcus said. "It gives me a wonderfully comfortable sense of being *padded*. It's like living in a quilted dressing-gown."

"That's all very well now. How will you feel when the weather gets hot?"

"Then I shall see it two-dimensionally, like a tapestry. It will luxuriate, it will leaf and flower, as the earth luxuriates outside."

About an hour before Ilse was due to arrive, Marcus found that Nancy had hidden the Jewish cookery book in a drawer under his shirts.

Only when the doorbell actually rang, and as he walked down to help the girl lift her trunk out of the taxi, did he remember that he had meant, at some moment when Nancy was not looking, to take the book out and place it in the empty wall bookshelf in the girl's room. Once the girl had arrived, it was too late. Her room became out of bounds to Nancy and Marcus. Even when the girl was absent, only the charwoman might go in.

Socially, having the girl was much easier than they had expected. Her English sounded abominable but she understood everything they said. She was excellent with the baby: not squeamish about its nappies; quick to accept the responsibility of deciding when to feed it. She gave it more to eat than Nancy did, because she had no worries about its weight. "I am being a fat baby, too," she said with complete self-complacency about her present figure, which was beautiful. The baby cried less. It became extraordinarily placid, smiled whenever it was awake, and grew fatter and fatter.

The three adults ate together in the kitchen. Ilse, although she was thin and tall—she was the tallest person in the house—liked to eat well. They quickly became informal, though not so intimate that either Nancy or Marcus wanted to let the girl know that Marcus was meant to be dieting; so, though he occasionally made token abstentions, Marcus ate well, too. They called each other by first names all round. Ilse laughed at Marcus's jokes. He made a lazy habit of decorously teasing her, which got them over such awkwardness as they encountered. Nancy could not bring herself to create a personal relationship with the girl, but only Marcus noticed her reserve. If she was not charming to the girl, she was thoroughly nice. She gave her the use of everything in the house, and was flexible and generous about time off.

Nancy lost her weariness, and Marcus lost his, which had been the weariness of feeling all the time that there was something he ought to be doing to help her. She recovered her good looks and her pleasure in making love. Marcus wondered if to feel her looks restored made her more confident in bed. They never made love with the romantic abandon he had once yearned for and failed to find, but he no longer yearned. The presence of the girl in the flat obliged them to take care not to make much noise; but it also released them because they knew that if, in their absorption, they failed to hear the baby cry, the girl would get up and go to it. In early May, Marcus made Nancy jokes, which also had a poetic content, about the phallic shape of chestnut candles; and when the candles had withered and the deep moist green leaves, losing the pleated look of the flesh on a baby's hands, opened to their fullest like the palms of hundreds of adult, caressing hands, he recovered his old, sensuously slothful feeling that, lying in bed with Nancy, he was lying roofed, shaded, enmeshed deep in summer greenness and could, with the least exertion but the maximum delighted consciousness, dip himself into what he lay beside, which could be compared to a warm pool or a book of poetry or a bag of chocolates.

By June, Ilse was coping so competently with the baby that Nancy decided to go back to work part-time. At first, ostensibly at least, she was merely replacing someone in the musical firm who was taking her summer holiday.

"How does it feel?" Marcus asked her, after her first day's work.

"Wonderful. I've got my identity back."

"Had you lost it?"

"Claire stole it, a bit."

Marcus noticed that the au pair girl, though she was efficient, was lazy. She was very desultory about attending her school. It surprised him in a German; but he supposed it was because she was beautiful as well as German.

She had remarkable auburn hair—deep brown shot with a colour he could only call orange—which she wore piled haphazard, with an effect of tribal aristocracy, on the top of her head, where she carried it as though it were a fine barbaric bit of native metal work. Her complacent appreciation of her whole body was like a primitive's physical pride.

The person Nancy was substituting for decided not to return to work after her holiday. Nancy decided to stay on.

The weather became hot. Marcus told Polydore that a heat-wave counted as a cold spell: he would stay at home, and the work must come to him.

The au pair girl began turning up her shirt and tucking it into the bottom of her brassière, so as to leave her midriff bare. One afternoon she appeared in the drawing room wearing a white bathing suit and told Marcus she was going to sunbathe in front of the window. She never asked permission to do things. She had left her hair loose, although, as Marcus told her (he had never seen it loose before), since it covered a good part of her shoulders, it would actually prevent her from getting suntanned.

He was working in the drawing room, sitting over some furniture.

The au pair girl folded a large towel in four, and, in the slightly disdainful way she did all physical actions, spread it on the floor and lay down, carefully disposing her hair at each side of her so that it did not screen her shoulders.

It was one of her afternoons on. Nancy worked a shifting timetable between mornings (in which case she left it to Ilse to give lunch to Marcus as well as the baby) and afternoons, and the girl's timetable shifted accordingly. The girl did not mind the shifts: they gave her a pretext for not going to school. And she preferred to be on in the afternoons, because then the baby was no trouble at all, sleeping in its big cot—it was not in length but in girth that it had quickly outgrown the carrycot—in front of an open window in the nursery.

"You and I and the baby," Marcus said to the au pair girl, without looking up from the intaglio he was contemplating, "are all lazy characters."

"Since I don't go to school today," she said, "I better do some homework."

After a minute or two she actually got up to fetch it.

As she passed Marcus, he put his hand out to her hair. He was careful to pull it, actually to hurt her a little, so that his gesture could still be passed off as a tease. Perhaps it was because of the pain that her head came round so swiftly towards his. Even as he drily brushed the surface of her mouth with his own he was still prepared to pretend, and still believed he could invent some way of maintaining that a kiss on the lips had no meaning; but she opened her mouth and with an astonishing swift violent voracity drew him in and, after interrupting him for a moment while she obliged him to close the curtains, drew him down on to the towel she had spread on the floor.

Thereafter they often made love in the afternoons.

Marcus felt pleased to be able to put it explicitly to himself that he had a mistress. It was almost as though he had become the sort of person Nancy had so long been urging him to be. Obviously, it was to Nancy that he really wanted to boast. Indeed, he knew he would tell her about it, though he might not word it as a boast, as soon as the au pair girl had gone—which would not be long; her immigration permit expired at the end of July.

He continued to think of his mistress as the au pair girl: *Ilse* continued to be reserved for his sister.

He never invited the au pair girl into his bedroom, and he took it that she understood he could not, since it was Nancy's bedroom, too. But neither did the au pair girl, although she had no corresponding reason, invite him into *her* bedroom. As her lover, he was admitted to her body; but evidently this made him not a bit the less shut out from her room as her employer.

Occasionally he felt apologetic towards the girl for his obesity: but she would be gone long before the strictest dieting could have made any noticeable difference: and anyway she was prepared to have him as he was.

Sometimes he tried to represent to himself the multifarious betrayals he was committing: of Nancy; of the girl, to whom he presumably stood in some parental, protective relationship; even—since the girl was employed to look after her—of the baby. But the girl was evidently beyond the control of any parent. And the baby was beneath the responsibility of any parent; she was not a personality, knew nothing, smiled and slept deep. She never once disturbed their lovemaking.

He was even less successful in needling his conscience

now than he had been about his father. Even the ultimate and quite artificial torture of putting it to himself that he was betraying his dead father failed to rouse him.

The July weather turned sulky. Marcus went back to work. In the end, when Ilse's permit expired, it was Nancy who saw her off in a taxi, with her trunk labelled "Hamburg". Marcus had carried the trunk down for them in the morning, and left it in the porch, then going up again for a moment to shake hands with Ilse.

When he came home again that evening, Nancy asked:

"Does the place feel empty?"

"I suppose so."

"Do you miss her?" Nancy said.

He thought to astonish and disarm her by going swiftly beyond her suspicions into certainty. "I always miss my bedfellows."

But she only nodded.

It was quite untrue that he missed Ilse at all: or, as a matter of fact, that they had ever been in a bed together.

Nancy had to take a week off work—it counted as her holiday—while they waited for another au pair girl. It made her irritable to look after the baby herself.

The day the new girl arrived—she was French—the hot weather began again. Marcus was not attracted by her. She had been with them only three days when she suddenly told Nancy she must go. She left that night: a friend would put her up, she said.

Nancy had suddenly to suspend work again. But, although it was so hot, Marcus decided to keep on going to Polydore's, where the basement was cool: and at home with the baby Nancy was continually impatient. "I get desperate when I'm cooped up with her all day."

After the French girl's departure Nancy said to him at dinner:

"When I first knew you, it was Rubens women."

"If you think I made a pass at the French girl, you're

wrong. I never looked at her. It must have been something else."

"What?"

"Perhaps she found out we're Jewish."

Towards the end of dinner he said:

"Why did you hide that cookery book in with my shirts? Did you want to impress it on my very clothing that I'm a Jew?"

"Don't be silly."

"Or are those colour plates your idea of art publishing?"

When he came home the next evening, Nancy said:

"*She's* been here."

"Who?"

"Ilse."

"Ilse?"

"I mean your sister."

"What did *she* want?"

"It's hard to say. Whatever she wanted, she didn't get it. It was absolutely loathsome."

"Why? I mean, why in particular? You usually find her visits loathsome, don't you?"

"She came to commiserate. Creeply-crawly. How in hell did *she* know there was anything wrong?"

"Did she? Is there?"

"Oh, she pretended it was because I'd had bad luck in losing my au pair girls."

"Well I daresay it *was*. She doesn't know of anything else. Don't get paranoid."

"Marcus, she seemed to be offering me herself as a substitute."

"Well maybe she thinks you're used to having an Ilse round the house. She only meant to be helpful, like most tiresome people. Actually, she'd make a hopeless au pair girl. She can't cope with Claire at all."

"No," Nancy said, agreeing, turning away. "But I meant, as a substitute for you."

On Saturday afternoon Nancy said:

"Do you mind if I take the chance to get out for a bit? Can you cope with Claire? She'll probably sleep anyway."

He sat for a while in the drawing room. It was too hot to work; and in any case—now that he had bound himself to stay in—the sunshine seemed to suggest that it would be ungrateful, even cruel, of him to let it go unappreciated.

He went into the bedroom to look for his bathing trunks, which he had not worn for years—not since he had given up holidaying with his sister. He found them under his shirts, under the Jewish cookery book. He could still get into them, because the material gave, but he bulged horribly through them.

He fetched a towel from the cupboard, laid it on the floor as Ilse had done and lay down to sunbathe in the drawing room.

When Nancy came home, which was earlier than he had expected, she found him standing in the corner of the drawing room looking at himself in a Victorian pierglass which Polydore had lately sent them.

"Baby all right?"

"Still sleeping," he said, still looking at his reflexion.

"You're disgustingly fat," said Nancy.

He made no reply.

"Just look at yourself," she said. "Look at your thighs. Look at your chest. You've got great pendulous breasts, like a woman."

He gave a chuckle. "It's a process of empathy. I've *become* a Rubens woman."

He repented it instantly and turned, quite quickly for him, away from the glass, meaning to go and put his clothes on.

But Nancy was in his way and she was staring at him in, he supposed, horror.

He stood still for a moment; and what he took to be the most awful, grossest insult to her of all was that her intent gaze at him was provoking the same effect on his flesh as she had once delighted to provoke in Lucca, where he had been thin.

He decided to hurry past her. But as he came up to her he recognised that her look was, in reality, desirous.

He did not know what to do. It was she who reached out to embrace him.

He pulled her down on to the sofa and after the first spasm of their embrace raised himself above her to examine her look. The effect of horror which he had originally expected *was* there, after all. It was simply that desire was there as well. Each caused the other.

The hostile and perhaps dangerous, perverted, situation between them prompted in him images of completely abandoned experience. But he was—because it was so hot, because he was married and at home, because he was so *fat*—too lazy. He began to make love to Nancy in his expert indolent way. She delighted him: and she groaned under the irresistible pleasure he caused her—and also because it *was* pleasure, because it *was* irresistible, where she might have preferred pain.

Perhaps her body was too nice to be pained. Anyway, he was too nice, and too lazy, to pain her.

Printed in Great Britain
by Amazon